A LETTER FROM THE
COLONIAL WILLIAMSBURG
FOUNDATION

Caesar was a real boy who lived on Carter's Grove Plantation in Virginia in the 1750s. He was a slave who belonged to the Burwell family. The other Burwell slaves who appear in this book also lived at Carter's Grove in the mid-eighteenth century.

Carter's Grove is eight miles southeast of Williamsburg, the capital of colonial Virginia. In the 1760s and 1770s, people in Williamsburg helped lead the thirteen colonies to independence.

Today, the Colonial Williamsburg Foundation teaches four hundred years of history at Carter's Grove. The slave quarter has been reconstructed to look the way it did during the second half of the eighteenth century. At the slave quarter and throughout the Historic Area in Williamsburg, people in costume tell the story of the African Virginians who lived as slaves in a society that valued freedom.

The Colonial Williamsburg Foundation is proud to have worked with Joan Lowery Nixon on the Young Americans series. Staff members met with Mrs. Nixon and identified sources for her research. People at Colonial Williamsburg read each book to make sure it was as accurate as possible, from the way the characters speak to what they eat to the clothes they wear. Mrs. Nixon's note at the end of the book tells exactly what we know about Caesar, his family, and Nathaniel Burwell.

Another way to learn more about Caesar's life is to experience Carter's Grove and Colonial Williamsburg for yourself. A visit to these places is a journey to the past—we invite you to join us on that journey and bring history to life.

D. Stephen Elliott
Vice President—Education
The Colonial Williamsburg Foundation

Read all the stories in the

YOUNG AMERICANS
_____

Colonial Williamsburg

SERIES BY JOAN LOWERY NIXON

Caesar's Story
1759

JOAN LOWERY NIXON

A Dell Yearling Book

35 Years of Exceptional Reading

Dell Yearling Books
Established 1966

Published by
Dell Yearling
an imprint of
Random House Children's Books
a division of Random House, Inc.
1540 Broadway
New York, New York 10036

Colonial Williamsburg is the trade name and registered trademark of the Colonial Williamsburg Foundation, a not-for-profit organization.

Text copyright © 2000 by Joan Lowery Nixon
and the Colonial Williamsburg Foundation
Photographs courtesy of the Colonial Williamsburg Foundation

Produced by 17th Street Productions

Visit us on the Web! www.randomhouse.com/kids

Educators and librarians, for a variety of teaching tools, visit us at www.randomhouse.com/teachers

ISBN: 0-440-41632-9

Reprinted by arrangement with Delacorte Press

Printed in the United States of America

July 2002

10 9 8 7 6 5 4 3 2 1

CWO

Contents

Prologue

"Hurry up," Keisha Martin called to Halim Jordan. "You want to hear Mrs. Otts's story, don't you?"

Halim shrugged. "I'd rather get something to eat."

"You can get something to eat later. Her story is going to be good."

"Yeah? How do you know that? You haven't heard it."

Keisha impatiently waited for Halim to catch up. "I know because I heard the first story Mrs. Otts told us, about Ann McKenzie. The next story she's telling us is about a boy who once lived near Williamsburg. He was a slave named Caesar."

"Yeah?" Halim began to look interested. "My

great-great-great-grandfather was a slave in North Carolina—"

"We know," Lori Smith interrupted. "You told Mrs. Hafferty in history class. That's why we thought you'd want to hear the story."

Keisha looked across Nicholson Street, beyond the wide green lawn of Market Square. "There's Mrs. Otts," she said. "She's packing up the things at her stall."

"Okay, okay," Halim said to Keisha. "I'm coming." He followed her to where some of the other kids from their class were gathered.

Mrs. Otts tucked one last ribbon-trimmed cap into her basket and smiled at them. Her brown-and-gray-streaked hair was neatly tucked into a ruffled white cap of her own, and she wore a flowered print dress. Like all the interpreters at Colonial Williamsburg, she was dressed in an eighteenth-century style.

"I'm heartily glad to see you again, dearies," she said. "You've come to hear about the young slave Caesar, have you not?"

Keisha nodded. "This is Halim Jackson," she said. "His great-great-great-grandfather was a slave."

"I'm glad to meet you, Halim," Mrs. Otts said. "Have you visited Carter's Grove plantation yet?"

"We're going there tomorrow morning," Halim answered.

For a moment sorrow darkened Mrs. Otts's eyes. "Then you'll not only see the grandeur of the mansion, but you'll also visit the slave quarter and discover how the plantation slaves lived."

Chip broke in. "Will we see their houses, too?"

"Yes, you will," Mrs. Otts replied. "And likely you'll remark how different they are from the mansion—which was called the *big house* in the eighteenth century—with its fine brick exterior and elegant interior. The slaves' homes were built of logs or wooden boards. Most of them were one- or two-room houses, with dirt or wooden floors. There were more male slaves than female slaves, so as many as five men without families often shared one of those small houses."

Stewart frowned. "How would they fit that many beds in a house?"

"Only some of them had beds, dearie," Mrs. Otts said. "The rest were given pallets to sleep on. The pallets were coarse linen cases stuffed with straw and cornhusks and could be rolled up during the day."

"They had tables and chairs, didn't they?" Lori asked.

Mrs. Otts shook her head. "Some did, and some

didn't. Many slaves lived at Carter's Grove. In one family, you might find that the husband had made a bed for himself and his wife and a table and chairs for the family. Another slave might have only a low three-legged stool or two. And another slave might not own any furniture at all."

"What *did* they have?" Lori asked.

"Well, they had pots for cooking hominy, from the dried corn they were given, and the vegetables they grew in their small gardens."

"What about meat?" Lori persisted. "Weren't they given meat?"

"Very little. Each adult probably received only one pound of pork, beef, or mutton each week. Many slaves supplemented their meat rations by trapping small animals—rabbits, opossums, raccoons, and squirrels."

"Did they hunt deer?" Stewart asked.

"The deer in this part of Virginia were mostly hunted out by the early 1700s," Mrs. Otts told him. "But in addition to small animals, there were turkeys in the forests and turtles, fish, oysters, and crabs in the rivers."

Halim scowled. "One-room houses with dirt floors, little or no furniture, and not much to eat! How did the slaves live like that?"

" 'Twas very hard for them," Mrs. Otts said, "but not because they had so little. Most of the people in the Virginia colony lived that way. Only a few people lived in the fine houses and had the luxuries you see in the Historic Area today. No, the hardest thing for the slaves was that they were not free. They knew that no matter how hard they worked or how obedient they were, they could be sold to pay a debt or hired out to earn the master some money. Even worse, they could not protect their family members from being sold or sent away. Even though slaves weren't allowed to marry, they were encouraged to have families because owners thought slaves with families would be less inclined to run away. A family that was large enough might have a house to itself."

"The slaves couldn't marry?" Lori's eyes were wide with surprise.

"They couldn't *legally* marry," Mrs. Otts explained. "But they had their own ceremonies, which to the slaves were every bit as binding, even though the owners didn't always see it that way. During the 1700s, when slaves married, there'd be a small gathering at night, and the man would give the woman a gift. Later on they worked out a ceremony called jumping the broom.

"Many slaves tried to make the best of their situation, but there were others whose hearts were so heavy at being separated from their families or having been treated harshly that they rebelled and ran away."

"That was a terrible way to treat people!" Chip said.

" 'Tis certainly true," Mrs. Otts agreed. "Unfortunately, slaves were considered property."

"What about the boy in the story you're going to tell us? Did he run away?" Keisha asked.

"Back in April of 1759 both Caesar and the heir to Carter's Grove, Nathaniel Burwell, had just passed their ninth birthdays. But then Caesar, who—as the saying goes—couldn't see an inch beyond his nose when opportunities arose . . ."

She paused and said, "Oh, dear. Pray excuse me for getting ahead of myself. Before I tell you what happened to Caesar, you should know that he was born on the large James River plantation known as Carter's Grove and lived in the slave quarter with his parents, Belinda and Sam; his older sister, Milly; and two younger sisters, Sukey and Nell."

Mrs. Otts leaned forward as she continued. "Sam, Caesar's father, learned the ways of carpentry. To be sure, very few carpenters in Virginia could turn out staircases and wainscotting any smoother or finer.

Sam had a real skill, and the overseers soon took note of it. A slave with a skill could be hired out, and was often given a small share of the wages he brought his master. Caesar was proud of the work his father could do, but he was lonely when his father was sent to work on other plantations or in Williamsburg— eight miles away.

"Milly was a pretty little thing who early on had been chosen to be a kitchen slave. Caesar, however, worked in the fields with his mother and Sukey, so he saw Milly only at nighttime when they were too tired to talk or play or do anything but sleep; and he missed the time he once had with her."

Mrs. Otts sighed. "As a fact, Caesar missed *everything* about his boyhood days. Until plantation children were about six, white child or black child, they had complete freedom to play. And often the master's children and the slave children romped together. But at some time between the ages of five and seven a big change came into their lives. The master's children began the education and training needed to manage the plantation, and the slave children were given jobs in the fields or the house, training for the work they'd do in the future.

"Unfortunately, Caesar didn't keep sight of his future. He kept glancing back at the freedom of his early childhood. I guess that was the start of all the trouble."

"Trouble? Please don't make us wait for the end of the story, Mrs. Otts. Tell us now. Nothing terrible happened to Caesar, did it?"

Mrs. Otts shook her head. "Be patient," she said. "Just keep in mind, the way we would like to end the story may not be the way the real story ended."

Chapter One

"Where do they come from—all those slimy tobacco worms?" Sukey asked Caesar as she squashed another worm and made a face. "Every day we turn each leaf, pickin' off the worms, but every day more worms come back. I ask you, where do they all come from?"

Caesar was too tired to smile at his seven-year-old sister's question. Along with the other slaves assigned to the large tobacco fields at Carter's Grove, he had spent a long day of stooping and squatting beside each young plant, turning the leaves one by one to pick off the worms and kill them. His legs, back, and shoulders ached.

This was Sukey's first year of work in the fields.

9

Picking worms was a chore even the younger children could do. "Ask Granny Hannah about the worms. She'll tell you," Caesar answered. He knew if Granny Hannah didn't have a story in her head about where worms came from, she'd make one up. Granny Hannah was so old she had no idea when she was born. She had long been assigned to care for the slave children under the age of seven while their parents worked in the fields. She loved to tell the children stories and legends from the African village where she had grown up.

Granny Hannah always began the stories by saying, "Remember what I tell you. All of us must keep rememberin', else we'll lose the stories forever."

"When can we go home? We been workin' all day, and I'm tired," Sukey complained.

Just then the overseer's deep voice rang out from across the field. Along with the other slaves, Caesar straightened, rubbing the small of his back. He smiled at Sukey. "Now we can go home," he said.

As they walked single file between the rows of plants, careful not to bruise them, Caesar thought about his own childhood, which had ended quickly when he reached the age of seven. He had been born just a week before Nathaniel Burwell, the master's son, and from the time they were four years old, the two of them had played together constantly.

Caesar clearly remembered one evening, after he and Nat had pretended to hunt for bears and wolves at the edge of the nearby woods. He'd flung himself into his mother's lap and happily announced, "Nat is my best friend."

Belinda had lovingly stroked his back, but at the same time had shaken her head. "Nathaniel is the master's son, and you are a slave," she'd said firmly. "You can never be friends."

"Yes, we can," Caesar had stubbornly insisted.

"You cannot, and it's time you learned that," Belinda had answered. Her voice was so tight and angry that Caesar sat up and looked into her eyes, but she didn't look at him.

"A friend is someone you can love and trust," she'd said bitterly. "He's not someone who buys you, owns you, and treats you as if you're not human."

"But Nat didn't do any of that. He's not to blame," Caesar had argued.

"Nat's no different from any other slaveholder," Belinda continued. She gripped Caesar's shoulder. "You'll never know how it is to live free, to go and come as you please, to own yourself."

"Like you did, Mam?" Caesar asked. Belinda

rarely spoke of her childhood, but when she did her words were filled with pain. He knew that another tribe had raided his mother's African village, captured her and others in her family, and sold them to slave traders.

"We were chained down in the hold of a ship," his mother had said. "We lay in pools of urine and vomit, sometimes terrified that the ship would sink and we'd be drowned." Her words had drifted into a whisper. "And sometimes, thinking of our future as prisoners forever, we *hoped* it would sink."

Caesar would never forget his mother's words, but he pushed the conversation out of his mind. He didn't want to hear anything against Nat. There was no boy he'd rather spend time with than Nat, and every day they eagerly ran to meet each other.

Caesar tried to be as much like Nat as he could. He whistled through his front teeth and he walked with his chin held high, just like Nat did.

Sukey teased him for "talkin' funny," and Milly complained, "Why you want to sound like the master's child?"

Caesar just grinned at his sisters. "I like the way Nat talks," he answered.

Caesar carefully kept the small, treasured horn-book Nat had given him in the shallow pit in the floor of their house, where the family kept what few valuables they owned. By Nat's side, Caesar had learned to read at the age of five.

Although many slave owners believed there was little value in educating their slaves, Carter Burwell had not objected. He also believed that all his slaves should be baptized in the Anglican Church and learn their catechism. So when Nat had begged that Caesar be allowed to learn to read with him, Mr. Burwell had told Nat's tutor he could include Caesar in the lessons. "Providing the boy seems able and interested," he'd added. Caesar had learned to read quickly.

Things changed, however, when Caesar and Nat were only six. Carter Burwell became ill and died.

After the funeral Nat was finally able to escape the crowd of people who had come to his home. Caesar ran with him to their special hideaway glen in the forest and sat quietly, holding Nat's hand and crying with him.

Then, when Caesar was seven, his life had altered forever. His playtime had come to an end, and he had learned just what it meant to be a slave.

"You're old enough now to begin to earn your keep," Mr. Ambrose Burfoot, the overseer, had told Caesar. He'd assigned Caesar to carry away armloads of brush and twigs that had been cut by the men clearing new land.

At the same time, Nat's guardian, his uncle William Nelson, decided Nat was at an age to begin learning the many duties involved in managing the large plantation, which now belonged to Nat and which someday he'd control.

At first there were many evenings in which Nat had sneaked down to the quarter to find Caesar. But Nat's studies had increased and Caesar's work hours had grown, and it had been harder and harder to find time to spend together. For two years Caesar had rarely seen Nat—and then only at a distance.

Mam was right, Caesar thought. Sorrow had squeezed his chest and throat as he fought back the hurt of what he'd become. *Nat is the master. I am a slave. We can never be friends.*

Sukey's shout broke into Caesar's thoughts. "Hurry, Caesar! Here comes Mam and Nell!" she cried. Sukey pushed Caesar aside and rushed past him to meet their mother on the road. Nell pulled away from her mother's hand and ran to hug Sukey.

"Mam, Mam!" Sukey yelled. "Those bad tobacco worms keep comin' and comin' and never stop!"

Belinda's smile seemed to erase the exhaustion on

her face. "Did you do a good job in pickin' 'em off today?" she asked as she pulled Sukey to her side.

"Yes, Mam."

Belinda looked to Caesar, and he quickly agreed, "She worked hard."

" 'Cept when I was tired," Sukey confessed. "Then Caesar helped me." She leaned against her mother as they walked toward their house in the quarter. "Why must I pick off worms?" she asked.

"Because it's the job given you to do," Belinda answered sharply.

Like his mother, Caesar knew there had to be a better way of life than slavery. He'd heard of slaves who had tried to run away, hoping to pass as free in the towns. According to Mr. Burfoot, most of them had been caught and punished. But, as the overseer continually reminded the slaves, punishment was not the worst thing a runaway slave faced. Mr. Burfoot's eyes gleamed as he talked of slave patrols capturing runaways and beating them so severely that the slaves died.

Caesar shivered, wishing he could get those stories out of his mind. Maybe they were true. Maybe not. Mr. Burfoot was mean enough to make them up just to scare people—especially the men who walked long hours on a Saturday night to visit their wives on other plantations. Caesar guessed that Mr. Burfoot wanted to make certain the men would return come Monday morning.

As they reached the door of their one-room log house, Caesar saw Milly standing in the open doorway.

"Milly!" he shouted, and ran toward her.

Milly's smile was wobbly, and as Caesar came close he could see that she had been crying.

"What's the matter? What happened?" Caesar asked, but Belinda stepped up and put a hand on his shoulder.

"Your daddy already told you?" she asked Milly.

Caesar saw the flash of bewilderment in Milly's eyes. He whirled toward his mother, his heart pounding with fear. "Told her *what*?" he demanded.

Belinda pushed them all inside the house. "Listen to me," she said. "We're proud of your daddy. He's bettered himself by learnin' to be good at a trade. Sometimes his extra pay has meant some beef or pork in the hominy pot." She waved toward the blankets neatly folded on top of the pallets they'd been given to lay on the hard-packed earth floor for sleeping mats. "It's meant that you sleep warmer in wintertime."

Caesar interrupted. "But what did Daddy tell Milly?"

"Hush, child, and let me go on with the rest of what I want to tell you," Mam said. "Your daddy's been hired out to a cabinetmaker name of Anthony Hay. This man needs skilled carpenters for some special work he's doing in Williamsburg. Skilled carpenters like Sam. He leaves tomorrow."

Sukey was the first to speak up. "Will Daddy be able to walk home on Saturday nights?"

"Don't count on seein' your daddy every Sunday," Belinda said.

Caesar looked at Milly. She had drawn back, her face bleak, her hands clenched at her sides.

"What's wrong, Milly?" Caesar asked.

Belinda glanced up at her eldest child. "Milly? Is somethin' else troublin' you?"

Milly took a deep breath, and her words came out in a rush. "I got some news, too, Mam. I won't be a kitchen maid any longer. I'll be a personal maid to Miss Lucy Burwell and learn how to do for her the way she wants."

Belinda sucked in her breath. "But that's fine news, child. I hear Miss Lucy has a kind nature. Of all those seven Burwell girls, she's said to be the gentlest. She'll treat you good."

Caesar stared at Milly. "That means you won't live with us anymore. You'll sleep at the big house."

17

Milly's face twisted as tears ran down her cheeks. "I'll sleep near my mistress. I won't see you or Sukey or Nell or Caesar, Mam."

"Hush, child," Belinda soothed. "We'll be right here near you."

"For now," Milly blurted out. "But what about later? Miss Lucy's nineteen years old. She's marryin' age. When she does marry and go away, she'll take me with her. I might never see you again!"

Belinda wrapped her arms around Milly and held her tightly, murmuring soft crooning noises against her hair.

Caesar noticed the tears on Mam's cheeks. He dropped to the dirt floor and sank his head into his hands. Daddy had been sent away on another job, and now Milly would live in the big house. No one in his family had asked to be slaves. They hadn't asked to have their lives torn apart by masters who decided where they should go and what they should do.

Why did things have to change? Caesar wondered. And why were the changes all for the worse? Why couldn't life be as easy and happy as it was when he was younger? There had to be a way of bringing back that happiness. But what could it be?

18

Chapter Two

That night, Caesar couldn't sleep. He saw his father, Sam, rise from the bed he shared with Mam and slip out the door. Quietly, so that he wouldn't wake his mother or sisters, Caesar followed him.

The night was chilly, with a breeze blowing off the wide James River. Caesar shivered, then ran to catch up with his father. Sam's broad shoulders and strong back were silhouetted against a bonfire. Caesar knew that on many evenings the men who were unable to sleep sat late around the fire and talked. Sometimes his father joined them.

This was a man's world, and Caesar had never tried to be a part of it, but on this night—his father's last night at home for a while—Caesar wanted to be with him.

When he reached the fire, Sam called out to him, patting a place on the log where he sat. "Come join us, son," he said.

Quick as a rabbit with a dog on its heels, Caesar scooted to sit by his father. He slid close enough to feel the warmth and strength of Sam's hard, muscular body. Quietly Caesar listened as the men talked.

"Mr. Burwell was a fair man," a friend named Gabe said. "He let you keep some of your wages when he hire you out. Now that Mrs. Burwell's relations has took over managin' the plantation, they fair with you?"

Sam nodded. " 'Bout as fair as I can expect. I get somethin'. It's not much, but at least it's somethin'."

"Huh. I'd rather stay in the fields than put extra money into somebody else's pocket."

Old Pompey spoke up. "Gabe's all talk, no sense. You did right to better yourself with your fine work, Sam. I heard on good authority you're thought of as the best carpenter in these parts."

"The best. That's right." The other men quickly agreed.

"Didn't say he wasn't," Gabe chimed in.

Caesar moved even closer to his father and leaned

against him. He was so proud of his daddy, he wished he were still a little child and could hug him.

The conversation then turned to the best ways to catch opossum. As Gabe and Turnus argued about which one had caught the most opossum, Caesar's eyelids began to droop. The next thing he knew, Sam was shaking his shoulder.

"Wake up, son," he said. "Time to walk home."

Exhausted, Caesar struggled to put one foot ahead of the other. In spite of his sleepiness, he was again filled with pride and love for his father. Daddy hadn't carried him as if he were a small child. He had made him walk, granting him the status of a man in front of the other men.

Caesar's determination grew as he thought, *While you're gone, Daddy, I'll do my best to take your place.*

Early Sunday morning, Caesar struggled from sleep. He was joyful because it was Sunday and the plantation field hands, after church services, would be given the rest of the day off.

But today Daddy is leaving, he suddenly remembered. Sorrow rushed through him. His father would be many hours away in Williamsburg.

The door of the house had been opened to let in

the cool morning air. Working by the light that came through the doorway, Caesar rolled up his sleeping pallet and stowed it in a corner. Then he ran outside to find his father, eager to spend every minute he could with him.

For the most part the quarter was silent, so Caesar trotted quietly across the path and up the ravine, where Sam stood, strong and still, a dark shadow against the pale sky.

Caesar rushed up, breathing rapidly. He wrapped his arms around his father's chest and held on as tightly as he could. "I don't want you to go so far away," he complained.

Sam put one arm around Caesar's shoulders. "Just be glad that I'll be workin' a fair-payin' job. I'll soon come home again, son," he said. "The Burwells have been good about keepin' families together. Some masters think nothin' of sellin' off a man, or his wife or children."

Caesar shivered, then nuzzled even closer to his father's side. "Milly was taken away from us."

"Only to the big house. That was a good thing for Milly."

"How can it be good to be sent away?" Caesar sighed. "It's best when we're all together each morning and night. I like it when I wake in the dark and hear you snoring and Mam puffing, and my sisters making little snuffling sounds in their sleep."

Sam chuckled. "You mean you like thinkin' back to when you was a child, still too young for breeches. You must remember, children grow up, things change. *I've* changed. I learned a skill, worked hard, and now I can earn money for the Burwell family and for myself. That's not a bad thing, Caesar. That's all to the good."

"But I liked it better the other way, Daddy," Caesar insisted.

Sam took Caesar's face between his hands and bent to look into his eyes. "You got growin' up to do, whether you like it or not, child."

He smiled and straightened. "Come on home with me. The sun's already dryin' up the grasses. It's time you get somethin' to eat and wash yourself. We'll soon be walkin' to Mr. Burwell's church."

The baptized Christian slaves on the Carter's Grove lands attended Sunday church services at the Chiscake Church chapel, attached to Yorkhampton Parish, because it was less than an hour's walk away. During the services, Caesar sat very still in the section for slaves at the back of the chapel. He tried to pay attention to the rector's sermon, knowing it would please his parents. Sometimes the sermons

23

were about Christ's life on earth, and the stories were interesting, so he didn't mind listening. But this morning the rector spoke about divinely ordained obedience—the colony's loyal obedience to the crown, a woman's obedience to her husband, and slaves' unquestioning obedience to their masters.

Caesar squirmed uncomfortably. From the Bible and the minister, he had learned that God loved the poorest slave just as much as the richest masters in the parish. If God saw no difference between Caesar and the Burwells, then why was Caesar a slave?

During the early afternoon, Caesar stayed close to his father's side, but soon Mr. Burfoot called Sam; the wagon was ready to take him to Williamsburg.

Sukey wrapped her arms tightly around Sam's neck. "Daddy, will you be back next Sunday?" she begged.

"I don't know, child," he said. "I'll have to walk from town out to the quarter, so don't count on seein' me every Lord's day. Just remember I'll do my best to come back as often as I can."

Belinda pulled Sukey away from her father. "Don't 'spect your daddy for the first week or two, at least. It always takes a little time to learn what's wanted."

Nell's mouth puckered, and tears rolled from her

eyes. "Daddy, tell them you want to come home," she wailed.

Mr. Burfoot called more loudly, "The wagon's ready and waiting, Sam. Come now."

"Yes, sir, Mr. Burfoot," Sam said.

Caesar ran to his father for one last hug. There was so much he wanted to tell him, but the words wouldn't come.

"I'll be home soon as I can," Sam said. He picked up the small bundle of clothing he had rolled inside a blanket and walked to the wagon without turning back.

Caesar ran inside their house. He couldn't bear to see his father leave, and he couldn't hold back the tears any longer. Now that it was up to him to help his mother and little sisters, he wouldn't let them see him cry.

Chapter Three

During the next week Caesar worked hard in the fields, sometimes along with his mother. And he doubled his efforts at home, trying to fill in the gap his father had left.

Nell was too little to help with the small vegetable garden Belinda had planted next to their house, and Sukey was usually exhausted after working all day in the tobacco fields. So Caesar weeded and tended the garden. He helped his mother prepare the fresh beans and field peas and pound and cook the dried corn kernels allotted to their family.

Sam had always added to their meals by trapping opossum or other small game and catching fish, so after his work in the fields was finished, Caesar tried to take on those jobs as well.

He walked into the woods, carrying an empty sack. With all his heart he wished he had paid attention the night Gabe and Turnus had bragged about trapping opossum. What had they done to catch so many? What had Daddy done?

As Caesar stood silently in the darkened woods, wondering what to do next, he heard a rustling in the tree over his head.

He stepped back and peered upward into the branches, trying to see what was making the sound. He thought he could make out the shape of a small animal. Was it large enough to be an opossum? Or was it a squirrel? There was only one way to find out.

He picked up a stone and let it fly, aiming at the shape over his head.

There was a thud as the stone hit the branch.

With a shower of leaves and small pieces of bark, the branch shuddered. Something flew from it, landed on Caesar's head, and bounced onto the ground.

"Ouch!" Caesar yelled. He rubbed his head where tiny claws had dug in, and watched helplessly as a squirrel ran into hiding.

He had no luck at catching anything that evening.

Caesar walked home discouraged. His stomach rumbled with hunger for the meat that Mam would have cooked if he'd been successful. Hominy was not enough. Vegetables were not enough.

Caesar met Gabe walking up from the river, half a dozen trout hanging from a string over his shoulder.

Gabe looked at Caesar's sack. "You been huntin'?" he asked.

Caesar shrugged and stared at the ground. "I didn't have any luck," he answered.

"Maybe tomorrow you can go with me," Gabe said. "You need someone to teach you—someone who knows how. But not Turnus. I'm the best, not him." He held up the string of trout, took the largest one off, and handed it to Caesar. "I've more'n I can eat. Give this one to your mother."

Caesar took the fish eagerly. "Thank you, Gabe!" he said.

Gabe chuckled as he walked in the direction of the small dwelling he shared with four other men. "Could hear that stomach of yours rumblin' clear down at the water's edge. Hate to see a growin' boy so hungry."

Later that evening, after supper, Caesar fought sleep. Gabe had helped him and offered to teach him to hunt. It was time, Caesar knew, that he took his daddy's place at the bonfire. There was much Gabe and the other men knew that he should learn.

As Caesar approached the fire, his heart beat rapidly. What if the men sent him home? What if they didn't accept him?

As he quietly slid onto the nearest log, a few looked at him and nodded a greeting.

Caesar relaxed, letting out the breath he had been holding. Turnus was talking about a free black sailor who had come to Norfolk from London.

"It don't happen often," Gabe said. "Matter o' fact, you like to never meet up with a free black man who's been to so many places."

"Stop interruptin' when I'm a-tellin' a good story," Turnus said. "I was about to say what this man said about London and the streets crowded with horses and coaches and people. Seems that . . ."

Warmed by the crackling fire, Caesar stopped listening and began wondering what it would be like to live as a free man, to travel and to stay where he pleased. But soon the deep voices and the wavering flames of the fire wove into a soothing, restful pattern of sound and light. Caesar fell asleep.

He awoke, lying on the ground, with his mother shaking his shoulder. The fire was out, the ground was cold, and Belinda was the only person in sight.

"Wake up, Caesar. Turnus said you were here. Come home to sleep," Belinda said quietly. "There's still a few hours left till daybreak. What are you doin' out here, anyway?"

Embarrassed, Caesar stumbled to his feet.

"Daddy sometimes sits with the other men at the fire."

"Your daddy's a grown man," Belinda said. With long strides she started up the ravine, and Caesar had to run to catch up with her. "You're only a boy. For now you sleep at home, not out here on the cold ground."

The next morning, as Caesar walked toward the fields, he had to put up with the grins and teasing of some of the men who had been at the bonfire the night before.

"Caesar! You get plenty of sleep last night?"

"You went to sleep before we got to some really fine stories, child."

Gabe shouted, "Ho, Caesar! I don't blame you for fallin' asleep. Turnus's stories get mighty dull. They'd put anybody to sleep."

Through the laughter that followed, Caesar felt his face burn. He kept his eyes on the ground and didn't answer. He wasn't angry with the men who laughed and teased him. He was angry with himself for not being able to fit into the empty spot his father had left.

On Friday Mr. Burfoot, the overseer, sent Caesar to till a field full of young tobacco plants. The workers were given hoes and lined up facing the north end of the field.

"Get those weeds out," Mr. Burfoot called. "Don't miss a one of them."

Caesar stood side by side with the other slaves between the rows of plants. It was the first time he had worked on a hoe gang.

"You're young, but you're big and strong," the overseer observed.

On either side of Caesar were two brothers, George and Tom. Grandsons of Granny Hannah, they had each reached the age of twenty and were grown men, but they'd always had time for Caesar, and he liked them.

" 'Twill be hot today," George said. He looked up at the sky, which was a flat, brilliant blue without a cloud in sight. "No rain today and tonight, for certain."

A triumphant look passed between the brothers that Caesar didn't understand. Why should they be so glad it wasn't going to rain?

31

At the end of the line a rich voice sang out, and Caesar grabbed his hoe, holding it high, as the others were doing. "Hoe, Emma, hoe!" the leader sang, and the rest joined in the song, their hoes chopping down, then up, in rhythm.

Setting the pace, the leader took the workers through the many verses of the song. Caesar sang, but he paid little attention to the words. Up and down, up and down, steadily the row of slaves worked their way across the field. Weeds were uprooted, and hard clumps of earth were shattered by the blades of the hoes. Caesar felt the sweat rolling down his face and stinging his eyes, but he knew better than to stop working to wipe his brow. Again he wondered what it would be like if he were free. What if this were his own field, if he could take pride in tilling his own piece of earth?

At midday a halt was called so that the workers could eat. It would be a short break, but enough to rest for a moment and find a bit of shade if they were lucky. Caesar wolfed down a chunk of corn bread, dipped the gourd into the water bucket for a drink, then headed for the woods that bordered the field. He skirted a tangle of shrubbery and walked deeper into the dimness, finding a shaded, grassy spot nearly hidden by the thickly grown trees. He stretched out, rubbing the sore muscles in his arms and shoulders, then lay quietly, trying to relax.

A nearby voice startled him. "We'll leave after dark. We'll make our way straight to Norfolk."

Recognizing Tom's voice, Caesar sat upright.

George spoke from the other side of the shrubbery. "We can pass for sailors. Who will say we're not free, if we say we are? We'll hire ourselves to a ship's captain and get away from this place."

Caesar gasped with surprise. Occasionally slaves ran away after a beating or to see family members who didn't live at the quarter. They always came back after a few days, even though they knew they would be punished. But were George and Tom talking of running away forever?

"What was that noise?" Tom whispered. His head appeared over the shrubbery. "Caesar! You was listenin'!"

Scrambling to his feet, Caesar protested. "I didn't want to listen. I couldn't help hearing you."

He joined the brothers, asking in wonder, "Aren't you scared to run? What if a slave patrol catches you?"

Tom's mouth was tight, and Caesar could see the fear in his eyes. "They won't catch us. We thought it all out. We know what to do to get away."

Caesar's hands trembled, and the hard lumps of corn bread in his stomach threatened to come back up. "If they catch you, they'll kill you," he said. "You heard Burfoot tell what they do to runaways."

But Tom looked at Caesar with eyes that seemed dulled with pain. "I used to be scared, but now it don't matter," he said. "Last week I got a beatin', and I promised myself there wouldn't be no more. I couldn't take another beatin', Caesar." He shrugged, turning away. "Besides, if they kill me . . . who'll care?"

George grasped Caesar's arm so tightly that it hurt. "Promise you won't tell on us," he insisted.

"I won't tell."

"Nobody. Not even your mother."

"Not even my mother."

George released Caesar, who rubbed his arm where George's fingers had dug in.

A sharp whistle sounded. Without another word Caesar, George, and Tom hurried to the field and took their places in line.

"Hoe, Emma, hoe." The leader began the chant, and the slaves took it up. *Raise the hoe, chop down with the hoe. Up and down, up and down. Keep the pace. Don't think. Just work. Don't think about what might happen to Tom and George.* "Hoe, Emma, hoe. Hoe, Emma, hoe."

Caesar was unable to follow his own advice. He couldn't help being frightened about his friends' plans to escape.

Chapter Four

It was early Saturday morning, as the slaves gathered for their assignments, when Mr. Burfoot discovered that Tom and George were missing. His eyes blazing with anger, the overseer ordered everyone to work. Caesar shook with such terror that it was hard to walk and even harder to raise his hoe.

The spots next to him were filled by other slaves. Knowing what he knew, Caesar didn't dare look up to meet their eyes or join in any of the whispering. Some of the slaves seemed worried, some hopeful, some frightened. Mr. Burfoot's stories had been very real. Terrible pictures flashed through Caesar's mind of men on horseback running down George and Tom.

"Hoe, Emma, hoe." As Caesar worked, the monotony, the pace, and the rhythm of the chant began to quiet his fears. The pictures in his mind changed to those of Tom and George on board a sailing ship—one even larger than those that came up the James River. They were smiling as they worked. They were laughing. They were free.

Caesar was swept with an intense longing to be free himself and for a moment wondered if he might run away to Norfolk, too, and become a sailor.

But other pictures crowded his mind—pictures of Daddy and Mam and his sisters. Could he leave them, even for the prize of freedom? No, he couldn't. He shook his head.

"Pay attention, child," whispered Jenney, who worked next to him. "Keep up with that hoe or you'll get us all in trouble."

When the whistle blew for mealtime, Mr. Burfoot appeared. His face stern, he motioned to the slaves to gather around. When they were all within hearing distance, he said, "The two slaves who tried to run away didn't get far. They both drowned as they tried to cross one of the rivers between here and Norfolk."

"Drowned!" Caesar cried out, then cringed as Mr. Burfoot turned his angry gaze on him.

"Let that be a lesson to all of you," Mr. Burfoot

37

said. "If the river didn't get them, a slave patrol would have. If any of you try what they tried, it'll be the end of you, too. Now eat, then get back to work."

Caesar looked at the lump of corn bread that was to be his noonday meal. He broke off a small piece and put it into his mouth, but he gagged and spit it out.

He felt a hand rest on his shoulder, and a soft voice said, "We don't know they drowned, child."

Caesar looked up into Jenney's sympathetic face. "Mr. Burfoot said they did," he protested.

"Mr. Burfoot say whatever he likes to say. Don't mean 'tis true. It mean the masters can't let us know their slaves got away. There be slaves who make their way to big places like Philadelphia or Boston or Charleston and pass for free, but their masters tell everybody they're dead."

The man next to her spoke up. "You're right, Jenney. They must say their slaves are dead, or other slaves might try runnin', too."

Caesar stared at them. "You mean all those slaves we heard about being killed really got away?"

"No, child," Jenney said. "Most runaways are caught. And some runaways are killed. Only a few make it to towns where they can pass for free. Even then, they live in dread that someone will come who will recognize them and send them back."

What Jenney had said didn't satisfy Caesar. He couldn't stop thinking about George and Tom. As he worked, nearly to sundown, he was filled with a terrible sadness, and he wished he could go back to his younger years when Daddy was home, and Milly slept in their house, and he and Nat seemed to have the whole world to play in and explore.

I must see Milly, Caesar told himself. *I want to tell her that I miss her.* His decision made him feel a little more secure.

After Caesar put up his hoe, he splashed cold water on his head and face and walked up the path to the laundry near the big house.

While he wondered if he should go inside, Judeth, one of the house slaves, staggered to the doorway with a large pan of soapy water.

She started when she saw Caesar and immediately demanded, "What you doin' here, child?"

"I came to see my sister Milly," Caesar said.

Judeth struggled through the door, then flung the water onto the ground. With one hand she smoothed her apron, tugging it back into place, and asked, "What you want to see her about?"

"I just want to see her," Caesar said.

"You can't do that," the woman said. "Milly's busy with Miss Lucy."

Caesar's throat grew tight, and tears burned behind his eyes. He took a step backward, but he said, "Can I see Milly some other time?"

"No," Judeth said. "Milly can't run off to see you whenever she wants. She works for Miss Lucy now, and Miss Lucy needs her at hand. Go along home with you, child, and don't come back. You don't belong here."

Sick at heart, Caesar turned and walked down the path behind the large Burwell house. For a moment he paused, feeling strange about being in this spot. It was as if someone were watching him, warning him to leave. The words kept repeating in his head: *You don't belong here. You don't belong here.*

Caesar's glance was drawn upward to one of the large windows over his head. Someone was watching him from the window. It was Nat and he was watching carefully.

Raising a hand in greeting, Caesar began to smile, but Nat stepped away from the window, disappearing from sight.

How could the boy who had once been his best friend not even acknowledge him? Caesar ran as fast as he could toward the slave quarter and home. What had happened to Nat?

As Caesar walked through the door of his family's house, his mother looked up from where she was seated on the floor, patching Nell's shift of unbleached linen.

"Will Daddy be home tonight?" Caesar blurted out. More than anything else he wanted his family around him. He wanted to feel safe and needed and loved.

Slowly Belinda stood and took Caesar's face between her hands. "No. You heard what he told us. I know how much you miss your daddy, but don't look for him comin' tonight," she said. "Or maybe for the next Saturday or the next. I told you, he must make a place for himself where he's workin'. He must find out what's expected of him. Your daddy will come as soon as he can."

Caesar's shoulders drooped. "I wish . . ." He stopped and said instead, "I'll go weed our garden."

Belinda hugged Caesar, then stepped back, smiling at him. "You been weedin' all day long," she said. "It will be light awhile longer. Why don't you see if you can catch us some fish for supper?"

"I'll try, Mam," Caesar said, feeling a little better. He'd much rather go fishing than fight more weeds.

He took the pole his father had made from a slender branch that he'd scraped smooth. A string had been fastened to the end of the branch. At the free end of the string was a small nail that had been pounded into a hook.

Along the way to his favorite spot, where he had often played with Nat, Caesar caught a few crickets and beetles to use for bait. He followed a narrow path through the woods that led downstream to a small cove sheltered by pines. Settling down on the bank, he put a cricket on his hook and dropped his string into the water. Maybe he'd catch a few croakers or even a trout or two.

As he heard footsteps behind him, Caesar jumped up and whirled around. His hook flew out of the water.

"Don't scare the fish or you won't catch any," Nat said.

"Nat, it's you!" Caesar said happily. Nat hadn't forgotten him. "I saw you in the window of your house. I started to wave, but—"

"Sit down, Caesar," Nat said.

As Caesar did, Nat sat beside him.

Caesar dropped his bait back into the water and

smiled at Nat. "I wish I had two poles so you could fish, too."

Nat gestured at his soft woolen waistcoat and breeches and spotless white shirt and stockings. "As you can see, I didn't come here to fish," he said.

For the first time, Caesar became aware of Nat's clothing. Dressed in the same kind of fine clothes his father had worn, he was a small image of Carter Burwell. All that was missing was the fancy wig most gentlemen wore.

Suddenly aware of his own heavy, rough linen trousers and stained shirt, Caesar looked away in embarrassment. He'd been growing. He was sure he was at least an inch taller than Nat. His pants were too short, and Mam had patched his shirt where it had worn thin. Caesar would have to wait until summer was over before his family would be given an allotment of cloth with which to make new clothes.

Nat didn't seem to notice Caesar's silence. His voice was sharp with excitement as he asked, "You came to the house to see Milly, didn't you?"

"Yes," Caesar said quietly, "but I couldn't." He stared at the water, wishing Nat would leave.

But Nat went on talking. "My sister Lucy likes Milly. Milly learns fast, and she's quick to obey."

Caesar didn't answer. Milly was smart and lively

and good-natured. She shouldn't have to run to obey Miss Lucy's commands.

Nat broke the silence. "Caesar, you and I had many good times together—some of them here in this spot. I remember when . . ." For a moment he hesitated. Then he said, "We were very young children. Uncle William has impressed upon me the fact that the past is over. Small children cannot understand that there are differences in position and in responsibilities that must be accepted."

Nat gave a little shake of his head, as if he were shaking all his thoughts into order. Then he smiled and said, "However, there can be better times ahead for both of us."

Caesar was puzzled by the excitement that sparkled in Nat's eyes. "What better times? What are you talking about?" he asked.

Nat grinned. "I need a personal servant, Caesar. Old Juba moves too slowly for my taste, so it's time to give him other work. I told my guardian that I want *you*."

Caesar knew his mouth was open, but he was too stunned to answer.

Eagerly Nat went on. "Uncle William thought you were too young. And he complained that you were a field hand and untrained for the job of personal servant. I knew he'd object, but he's fair and willing to listen to reason." He laughed. "You might say I kept 'reasoning' until he finally gave in."

At last managing to find his tongue, Caesar said, "Nat, I—"

Nat interrupted. "That's *Master Nathaniel,* Caesar. We'll start your proper training right now."

Caesar tried to gulp down the lump that was clogging his throat. Quietly he said, "Master Nathaniel, I can't be your personal servant. My daddy has been hired out as a carpenter in Williamsburg, Milly's no longer at home, and I have to care for my mother and little sisters."

Nat seemed puzzled as he shook his head. "No. You do not. They live better than most slaves. They have a house to themselves, clothes to wear, enough hominy to eat, and the overseer will watch out for them. They won't need you there."

Caesar knew he shouldn't allow himself to show his feelings. He shouldn't raise his voice. But he couldn't help it. "Somebody has to help work the garden, and trap a rabbit or 'possum now and then for dinner." He waved his fishing pole for emphasis. "Mam can't do that and cook and work the fields and take care of the little children, too. She needs me."

At first Nat frowned. Then he looked at Caesar

patiently and spoke firmly. "Caesar, my uncle William has taught me to always remember that slaves don't have the ability to make intelligent choices. Their masters are obliged to make decisions for them. I've given this matter a great deal of thought, trying to make the right decision, and I believe that I know what is best for you."

He stood and once again smiled happily. "You'll be given some proper clothing to wear, and Old Juba will be assigned to teach you what to do and how to behave as a manservant. This is a fine opportunity for you, Caesar, and I'm sure that when the surprise wears off, you will be properly grateful."

Caesar stood, too, eyes downcast, until Nat strolled away. Heartsick, Caesar released his bait, pulled his pole from the water, and ran toward home.

Chapter Five

Belinda listened wide-eyed as Caesar, with tears running down his cheeks, told about his meeting with Nat. Belinda gathered him into her arms, soothing him until his sobs turned to dry shudders.

"Master Nathaniel was right," she said. "This is a fine thing happenin' to you."

Caesar pulled back, stunned. "You want me to leave, like Milly did?"

"No, I don't want you to leave," Belinda whispered. She rubbed the back of one hand across her eyes and sucked in a shuddering breath.

Finally she spoke again. "You're my only son. You don't know how much I'll miss you. But I want you to have the best that can come to you," she said quietly. "There'll be plenty of work, bein' a personal servant, but it's nothin' like the backbreakin' work you'd have to do in the fields."

"I told Nat—Master Nathaniel—that I wanted to stay with you," Caesar said.

Belinda, her eyes wide and frightened, grabbed Caesar's shoulders. "Oh, child, you didn't!"

Grumbling, Caesar said, "Nat told me slaves didn't have the ability to make intelligent choices so he had to make my decisions for me."

"Let him!"

Caesar stared at his mother in bewilderment. "You want me to do everything Nat says and not tell him what I think?"

Sighing, Belinda let her hands drop. "Remember, child, if you anger your master, you can be sent far away to work in other fields, or you can be sold. You don't know how horrible an auction block can be."

"Is that how you were sold, Mam?"

"Yes, it is," Belinda answered. "When our ship arrived in Virginia, all of us prisoners were led onto the dock in chains—like animals. Then, one at a time, we were brought out to stand on a block where white people could inspect us. I was a young girl. I didn't understand the language the auctioneer was saying. But I heard people laugh, and I saw how some of them looked at me."

"Oh, Mam," Caesar cried. He gripped his mother's hand.

"I was lucky that I was bought for Carter's Grove," Belinda said. "I haven't been mistreated here, as I might've been elsewhere. There are some places where slaves live every day of their lives knowing that at any moment they can be whipped—or even killed—at the whim of their masters."

She took a deep breath and straightened her shoulders. "I do not want you to be sent to the auction block, child. So—no matter how you feel—you must behave to white people as I have always taught you."

"But Daddy's been sent away and—"

Belinda interrupted. "Hush now. Your daddy will be mighty proud of you when he gets home and finds you're workin' at the big house. Don't you see? He worked hard to learn special skills so we could live better. You'll do the same as him. Bein' a personal servant takes special skills, too. You do this job for your daddy and me, child, and do it well." She hugged Caesar again.

Aching inside, he gave in. There were no tears left to cry, no choices left to make. He felt like a dried leaf, blowing in the wind, unable even to choose where to land.

Will my life always be like this? he wondered. A stubborn voice in his mind answered, *Not if I can do something about it.*

On Sunday morning, Caesar washed and dressed in clothes that had been scrubbed and boiled until they were faded and thin in spots. He and his mother and sisters walked to the Chiscake Church for services. This time the rector spoke about God's great love for all mankind.

Caesar sat quietly, staring down at his hands. He hoped the rector was right. He wanted God to love him. But had God ever been a slave? Did he know how slaves felt? The white people in the church heard the same words from the minister about God's love for everybody. Caesar wondered how they could believe in that love and still own slaves. He also wondered: If he asked God to help him and his family to someday be free, would God listen? Would he help?

After services, Caesar walked home with his family. As they came near the quarter, Gabe walked out of the house he shared with some of the male slaves. He held some empty hemp sacks in his hands.

Smiling, Gabe greeted Belinda, spoke to Sukey, and patted Nell's hair. Then he turned to Caesar. "Seems time to show you how to catch 'possum," he said.

Caesar's heart gave a jump. "Yes! I want to learn!" he said.

"It's easy. Those old 'possums are just waitin' to be caught," Gabe said. "Come on. I got some sacks and some bait. That's all we need."

Caesar looked to his mother. Belinda smiled at him. "Run along, child. Get us a 'possum for supper. And say 'I thank you' to Gabe."

As they walked into the woods, Gabe said, " 'Possums like to eat eggs and fruit the way I like to eat sweet cakes. I got some dried apples—don't ask where. We go to where those 'possums are hidin' up in the trees, layin' low. We put our apples on the ground, get behind some bushes, and wait."

"I can climb the trees to get them," Caesar offered.

"No need to climb no trees. The 'possums will come down to get the apples. Then we jump out. They drop over, pretendin' to be dead. That's what 'possums do when they scared, like that would fool anybody with any sense. We just pick those old 'possums up by their tails and drop 'em in our sacks."

Quietly Caesar followed Gabe farther into the forest. As they reached a small clearing, Gabe stopped so suddenly that Caesar ran into him.

Gabe held a finger to his lips. Then he pointed upward.

Caesar peered through the thick leaves of the nearest tree. He was able to make out an opossum hanging from a branch.

Gabe motioned to Caesar to stay where he was. Then he quietly moved ahead, placing the fruit on the ground. Even from where he stood Caesar could smell the spicy, tart fragrance of the wrinkled red apples. He wondered if the apples were from the Burwell storeroom. It would have been very risky for Gabe to take them, but he wouldn't have been the first slave to give in to temptation and help himself to a few apples.

Gabe then sidled behind a clump of shrubbery. He motioned to Caesar to join him, and when Caesar did, Gabe handed him an apple to eat.

"What do we do now?" Caesar whispered to Gabe.

"We wait," Gabe said. He suddenly smiled and pointed to the trunk of the tree. Two fat opossums were slowly climbing down, on their way to the stash of apples.

As the opossums pounced on the apples, holding them tightly in their tiny paws, Gabe whispered, "Let 'em enjoy a few bites. 'Tis the last thing they'll eat 'fore we eat them."

He climbed to his feet, and Caesar hopped up, too, quickly taking the sack Gabe thrust at him. "Now, let's give those 'possums a good fright," Gabe said.

Gabe ran into the clearing, his big feet making plenty of noise. Caesar dashed after him, shouting.

The two opossums flopped over, trying to look dead, but Gabe and Caesar grabbed their tails and dropped them into their sacks. Then they picked up the apples, found a new spot, and tried it again. This time they caught three.

"That's enough for now," Gabe said. "We ought to get back. Next time you try this by yourself, get a couple of eggs. 'Possums like eggs, too, and they're easier to come by."

Caesar grinned at Gabe. He'd had a wonderful time. "Thank you, Gabe," he said. "We'll have a good supper tonight."

"My pleasure to do somethin' for Sam's boy," Gabe said. "Your daddy's a good man."

"Yes, he is," Caesar said happily. "But it's hard to take his place."

"You can't never take his place," Gabe answered. "In this life everybody must make his own place."

On the way home Caesar thought about what Gabe had said, but he was puzzled. How could he make his own place if he had no say about it? How could any slave make a place of his own?

Chapter Six

The next morning Mr. Burfoot ordered Caesar to remain behind when the others walked to the fields to work. Grumbling under his breath, the overseer made certain that Caesar was well scrubbed. Then he handed him a plain white shirt, a pair of brown knee breeches, white stockings, a collarless brown jacket, and a pair of new shoes.

Caesar's old shoes were worn and soft, and as he slipped the new pair on over his feet, he cried out.

"They can't be too small," Mr. Burfoot said. "To be sure, they seem a bit overlarge to me."

Caesar tried to take a few steps and stumbled. "It's hard to walk in these shoes."

"You'll get accustomed to 'em," Mr. Burfoot growled. "Stop limping. I don't want to hear no complaints from you. You do as you're told up there. Understand?"

"Yes, sir," Caesar answered. Reluctantly he trudged up the path. He looked back over the road to the woods where he had once played with Nat. During the happy days of his childhood, he hadn't realized what it would be like to be a slave.

Old Juba greeted Caesar as he stepped into the kitchen. Then he started teaching Caesar about his new duties as a personal slave.

"You've gotten an important job here in the big house. Master Nathaniel's learnin' what to do when he's grown and owner of this plantation," he told Caesar. "Part of that learnin' is knowin' how to take proper care of all his slaves—not just house servants but field hands, too. You can help him with that part."

"Me?" Caesar answered in surprise. "How could I help him learn that?"

"If you're polite and courteous and respectful to your master, it encourages him to be the same to you . . . and to others."

This was strange advice, and Caesar had to think about it. He and Nat had been close friends. They had pretended to hunt bears together, they'd rolled down hills together, and they'd chased and wrestled and laughed together. You didn't have to think about being polite and courteous and respectful to a good friend. You just felt good being together.

Old Juba waited patiently, then said, "You'll be given a new pallet. Each night you'll sleep on the floor by the fireplace in Master Nathaniel's chamber. If he calls you, no matter what time it is, go to him, fast as you can. Maybe he'll want a glass of water or maybe he'll just want to know someone's there. Lately he's been havin' bad dreams that worry him. In any case, whatever he says to do, you do it right away."

Caesar frowned. He didn't like the idea of getting up in the middle of the night when he'd rather be sleeping. "What if I don't wake up when he calls?"

Old Juba gave Caesar a firm look. "You learn to wake up," he answered.

Old Juba taught Caesar how to care for Master Nathaniel's clothes, how to brush them and fold them and keep them free from dust in the clothes press. And he showed him how to lay out what Master Nathaniel was to wear each morning. He instructed him to keep the bottle in the bedchamber filled with fresh water and the basin spotlessly clean. And he told him to be sure to warm the water on a chilly morning.

Old Juba went over and over all Caesar's new duties, right down to the smallest ones, such as making sure there were fresh candles in the polished candleholders and a supply of both logs and kindling stacked in the service yard behind the house.

Old Juba worked with Caesar for a few days, sometimes standing quietly in the background as Caesar took care of Nat's needs. But at night Caesar was alone with Nat, and Nat sometimes awakened, crying out, trying to separate his dreams from reality. He'd sit up, rubbing his eyes or holding his head.

"Do you want to tell me of your bad dream?" Caesar asked.

Nat would always shake his head. "No," he'd say. And often he'd mumble to himself, "There is too much to learn." Or "I don't wish to be cross, like Uncle William. I wish to be like my father."

Caesar didn't understand. He would have liked to help Nat chase away his bad dreams, but he didn't know how.

One evening near the end of the week, when rain battered the windows of Nat's chamber, Caesar lit a cozy fire in the fireplace. He stepped back, watching the flames.

"It makes me think of the bonfire my daddy built for us one night," he said to Nat. "Remember? He told us that story about the skeleton head in the woods, and we both got scared and kept looking over our shoulders into the dark."

Nat laughed. "I remember. And the next day we pretended that the old skeleton head was after us."

"You got scared," Caesar said.

"No, I didn't. You did."

"Not me. It was you."

"Was not!"

"Yes, it was, 'cause I hid behind a tree and jumped out shouting and you yelled and took off running, like this—"

Caesar dodged to the right, throwing his arms wide. Too late he realized that he had struck a vase of flowers. He grabbed for it, but it crashed to the floor.

"What sort of hubbub is this?" a deep voice asked.

Caesar whirled toward the doorway to see William Nelson. Nat's uncle and guardian was tall and broad-shouldered. At the moment his fists rested on his hips and he glared at Caesar.

"I—I'm sorry, Master Nelson," Caesar stammered. His heart pounded, and he was so frightened it was hard to see.

Mr. Nelson stared at the broken vase, the scattered flowers, and the puddle of water that was spreading over the floor. "Was this breakage deliberate? Or was it a careless accident?" he demanded.

Nat spoke up first. "It wasn't deliberate, Uncle," he said. "It was an accident."

Caesar was unable to speak. He could only nod.

"I'm glad it was not deliberate, but I do not accept carelessness, either," Mr. Nelson said to Caesar. "There are too many so-called accidents of this sort around this house. Perhaps a whipping will help you be more careful in the future. And it may remind others as well."

A whipping! Caesar's knees wobbled, and he reached for the back of a chair to steady himself. He had seen slaves who had been beaten, tied to a post where all could watch, their backs cut and bleeding from the stinging lashes. He tried to speak, but he was so frightened that no words came from his mouth.

Again Nat spoke up. "I pray, Uncle, that you will reconsider," he said. "Caesar knows now what the punishment will be if he is careless again. You can see how frightened he is. I am sure that the warning will be a sufficient lesson."

"You are very much like your father, Nathaniel," Mr. Nelson said. "But I'm afraid that Carter Burwell was far too lenient toward his slaves. I have learned from experience the importance of strong discipline, corporal punishment, and separation of families. Caesar's training can only be helped by the administration of a firm hand."

Nat held his ground. "You have given me the responsibility of training Caesar," he argued. "Whether or not his actions merit punishment should be *my* decision."

Mr. Nelson scowled at Caesar before he finally answered. "Very well, Nathaniel. You have taken on the task of training him. I bow to your judgment."

"Thank you, Uncle William," Nathaniel said.

Caesar gulped, nodded, and managed to whisper, "Thank you, sir."

As soon as Mr. Nelson had left, Caesar turned to Nat. "Thank you, Na—Master Nathaniel," he said.

He expected Nat to smile, maybe even joke, but Nat's expression was stern. "Clean the floor quickly, Caesar," he said. "When you've finished, prepare my chamber. I wish to retire early."

"Yes, sir," Caesar said, but Nat had already turned his back and was walking out of the room.

Suddenly Old Juba was at Caesar's side with cloths and a small basket. Silently he helped Caesar pick up the broken vase and flowers and mop up the water on the floor. As Caesar began to carry the basket downstairs, Old Juba drew him aside into an empty room.

In the darkness Old Juba spoke so quietly that Caesar strained to hear what he was saying. "You can make your life much easier, child, by payin' attention to the rules."

"I wasn't breaking the rules," Caesar insisted. "I was just showing Nat—Master Nathaniel—how he ran when he thought the skeleton head in the woods was after us when we were children."

"I was nearby. I heard what you was sayin'."

"We were just having fun remembering."

"*You* may have been having fun, but not Master Nathaniel. He didn't like being told he was scared and you weren't."

Surprised, Caesar answered, "But he *was* scared."

"No matter if he was or not. You did yourself no good by telling him so."

"I thought—"

Old Juba shook his head. "That's the trouble, child. You *didn't* think. You didn't 'member what you learned from that story. Your daddy told you the story about the slave boy and the skeleton in the woods for a reason. Stories are a way that fathers and mothers teach their children. The old skeleton head told the boy, 'Mouth brought me here, and it gonna bring you here, too.' Remember? The boy runs to his master, gets him out of bed, and leads him to the forest. Master don't like gettin' out of bed, so he tells the boy, 'If you lyin' to me, it will be the last lie you tell.' When the master's there, the boy can't get that old skeleton head to talk, so the master does what he said he'd do. After the master goes away, the skeleton head says to the poor, dead boy, 'I told you . . . mouth brought me here, and it gonna bring you here, too.' Didn't your daddy tell you what that story mean?"

Caesar's forehead puckered as he tried to remember.

Old Juba sighed. "It mean you don't say all you see, and you don't tell all you know."

"I remember now. That's just what my daddy said."

"That's right," Old Juba continued. "An' didn't your mother teach you to have two faces? You put on your own face for your own people, but you put on another face for white people. You look down, you speak soft and polite, and you hurry to do whatever they ask—no matter what. It's the only way you'll last, Caesar. Life is hard enough. There's no sense in your makin' it any harder."

"But Nat and I—"

"That part of your life is over. You must forget it.

63

You have a master you want to serve the best you can. Keep that in mind. That's all that counts for you."

With a heavy heart Caesar nodded. He knew that what Old Juba had told him was true.

Old Juba reached for the basket. "I'll take this. You hurry back to your master, child. Speak humbly, and do for him the way you should."

"I will," Caesar said. "Thank you." He ran to Nat's chamber.

Nat was already there, dressing for bed. Caesar turned down the quilt, smoothed the sheets, and fluffed the pillows. He neatly folded Nat's clothing, after brushing the breeches and coat, and buffed Nat's shoes. Then he checked under the bed to make sure the chamber pot was there. One morning he'd forgotten to return it after he had completed the unpleasant task of emptying it and washing it. Caesar remembered how angry Nat had been when he couldn't find the chamber pot during the night. He didn't want that to happen again, especially when he had just escaped a whipping.

As Nat climbed into bed Caesar asked politely, "Will there be anything else, Master Nathaniel?"

For the first time since the vase had broken, Nat looked into Caesar's eyes. He pulled the quilt up to his chin and muttered, "*I* wasn't the one who was scared in the woods. *You* were."

Caesar stood as tall as he could and took a long, deep breath. He looked down at his feet. "Yes, sir. You were right. I was the one who was scared," he said.

I said it, humbly and politely, without choking, Caesar thought, but there was a hollow in his chest, as if a piece of him had been torn out, because what he'd said wasn't true.

During the night the wind died down. Caesar lay on his pallet, watching the glow of the banked fire, unable to sleep. *What will it be next time?* he wondered.

He shivered and rolled over, turning his back to the fire, trying to suck in the remaining warmth. He'd have to be very, very careful that there wouldn't be a "next time."

Chapter Seven

For the next few weeks Caesar put into constant practice the proper manners Old Juba had taught him. His chores kept him so busy he rarely found time to talk with Milly.

Sometimes they met on errands to the kitchen, and Caesar was sure his smile was always as broad as his sister's. Occasionally he saw Milly at Burwell family gatherings, when she attended Miss Lucy and he stood ready to fulfill Nat's requests. Each time their eyes quickly met, and Caesar was content.

Just as Old Juba had instructed Caesar, Milly was quick to take care of Miss Lucy's needs and wishes, and her gaze was always directed downward in a submissive manner.

Caesar knew he should be proud of her, but sometimes he wanted to cry out in protest. That quiet, meek girl wasn't Milly! Milly was quick to laugh, bright-eyed, and lively. It made Caesar ache to see Milly as she acted in the big house—a Milly he didn't know.

However, Caesar remembered the beating he had narrowly missed, and he was well aware of the line he should not have tried to cross. Ever since that night, Nat had spoken formally and impersonally to him. Whatever might have been left of the friendship they had shared as young children seemed to have disappeared.

Caesar was careful to put on his well-practiced "other face" and to be courteous and respectful whenever he served Nat or was with the Burwells and their guests.

But one warm Saturday evening, when the ground steamed from a two-day rain, and vapors rising from the wet grass spiced the air, Milly pulled Caesar aside. "Daddy's walked home," she whispered.

Caesar started. "Daddy's home? For good?"

The other slaves, who happened to be in the kitchen, turned to stare.

Milly rested her fingers against his lips. "Hush!" she commanded. "No. He finished the first job three weeks ago. Since then he's been on another."

Caesar pulled away. "How do you know? Have you seen him?"

"Someone told Patt, the cook, and she told me. I didn't see Daddy, and I won't be able to go see him." She paused. "And neither will you—not with the dancin' master here and guests comin' to dance tonight and all Miss Lucy and Master Nathaniel needs for us to do."

"I'll ask Master Nathaniel if he'll let me go."

"You can ask. Won't do no good. You've your duties here to keep you busy."

Stubbornly Caesar said, "I want to see Daddy."

Milly sighed. "I shouldn'ta told you." She frowned at Caesar and tapped him on the nose with one finger. "Don't you get foolish notions about goin' to see Daddy. You tend to what your master tells you to do. You hear me, Caesar?"

"I hear you," Caesar mumbled, but his heart pounded with excitement. Whether Master Nathaniel gave him permission or not, Caesar was determined to get down to the family's house in the quarter and see his father.

Milly left the kitchen, carrying a cup of tea up to

Miss Lucy. Caesar turned to leave, too, but he saw Old Juba watching him, a sorrowful look in his eyes. Caesar snatched up the plate the cook had prepared for Nat and hurried back to the big house. One lecture was enough. He didn't want another one from Old Juba.

Caesar bounded up the back stairs and down the passage. Smiling, he burst into the back parlor—the second-floor room the Burwells used when they didn't have guests. He had left Nat there reading.

"Master Nathaniel," he cried out, "my daddy's walked home. He's here at Carter's Grove!"

Nat looked up, surprised, but he didn't ask about Sam. Instead, Nat sat next to the small table and focused his attention on the plate in Caesar's hands. "What did Cook send me?" he asked eagerly.

Caesar set the plate before him, and Nat smiled, rubbing his hands together. "Good," he said. "This should keep me from getting too hungry before supper is served."

Trying again, Caesar said, "Master Nathaniel, about my father . . ."

"Yes, you told me," Nat said. He picked up a slice of apple and took a careful bite.

For a moment Caesar thought of the opossums and how they bit their apples in the same way. Ever since that night, he'd wanted to tell Daddy how Gabe had taught him to catch opossums. Now he'd have the chance.

"Lay out my embroidered waistcoat with the blue frock coat and breeches," Nat said between munches. "And the shoes with the gilt buckles. There will be important people at the assembly tonight. My mother has informed us that it will be a special occasion."

"Yes, Master Nathaniel," Nat said. "May I have your permission to go down to the quarter tonight to be with my father?"

Nat stopped eating, surprised. "Tonight? How can you ask when you know that I may need you?"

"After the assembly?"

"It will be very late when the assembly is over," Nat explained. "Since your father has walked hours to get here from Williamsburg, I daresay he'll be tired, and you'd find him sound asleep."

Caesar's stomach hurt, and he felt sick inside. "I don't understand, Master Nathaniel. You won't give me permission to see my father?"

"Not tonight. You don't understand, but things like assemblies must be done properly," Nat said. "I'm sorry, Caesar." For a moment he truly looked sorry. Then he said, "Oh, Caesar, don't you realize how it

70

will look to my family and our guests if I am not attended by a personal servant tonight? Uncle William is watching closely to make sure I am training you well. If he were to think my training was amiss . . ."

Nat turned away and picked up a small wedge of cheese, popping it into his mouth. He licked his fingers and asked, "May I have a damp cloth, Caesar?"

"Yes, sir," Caesar said. He quickly dampened a soft cloth with warm water and carefully wrung it out.

As Nat wiped the cloth over his chin and hands, Caesar stood as tall as he could. Was Nat sorry because Caesar couldn't visit his father? Or was he concerned only about himself and staying in his uncle William's good graces? *It doesn't matter*, Caesar thought. He promised himself, *I don't care if you give permission or not, Master Nathaniel. Tonight I will see my father.*

Whenever Caesar attended Nat at social gatherings, he kept his eyes on Nat, anticipating his wish for food or drink or something from his chamber. That night, however, Caesar's thoughts were centered on his father. While Nat helped Mrs. Burwell greet her guests, Caesar stood quietly near the staircase at the back of the hall, planning exactly how he would sneak away from the big house to see Daddy.

71

When he had settled on a plan, he began to pay attention to the conversation around him. Often he heard something interesting. Sometimes there was something new to learn.

One of Mrs. Burwell's guests complained about the British government's interference with Virginia's laws. "They undermine the authority of the Virginia legislature," he stated.

"I agree, sir," another gentleman said. "Most especially in reference to our use of paper money. There is no excuse, sir, for not allowing us to pay our debts with our own money. No excuse at all! Virginians should have the freedom to make our own decisions."

Freedom? Caesar thought. *Does this man, who must own a great many slaves, have any idea what it's like not to be free?*

A portly gentleman took the other side, arguing for the position of the Crown.

Normally Caesar would have listened eagerly, remembering each scrap of information; but he stopped listening as the conversation went on and on. His breath came quickly, and his heart pounded. He was impatient to see his father.

It was late—very late—when Nat finally settled

down in bed. Caesar curled up on his pallet, listening intently until Nat's breathing became slow and steady. Good! Nat was asleep!

As quietly as he could, Caesar crept out of the room, across the passage, and down the back stairs. He opened the door and stepped out into the night. The stars were bright in a clear sky, and the world was so still that Caesar could hear the ripples on the banks of the James River below.

As Caesar stepped down the stairs, a soft voice said, "Stop where you are, child."

Startled, Caesar tripped and nearly fell.

A hand gripped his arm, steadying him. Caesar looked up into Old Juba's face. "Best thing for you to do, child, is go straight back upstairs to your sleepin' place."

"I want to see my father," Caesar insisted.

"What if Master Nathaniel wakes and finds you gone? You're sure to get a whippin'."

Caesar gulped down the lump that rose inside his throat. His body began to tremble. "I thought about being whipped, and the thought scares me. I surely don't want a whipping. But I'm willing to get one to spend a few minutes with my father."

Old Juba nodded. "You think they stop with you?

They most likely will whip Sam, too. And maybe even Belinda, if they think your mother and father encouraged you to run to them."

Caesar gasped in shock, stumbling backward. "No! They wouldn't."

"Didn't say they would or wouldn't. I said 'tis likely. It all depends on how the masters feel next mornin' when they wake up. They might be angry and might want to set an example."

"So 'tis their decision."

"No, child," Old Juba said softly. " 'Tis yours."

Caesar shuddered. "I don't want Daddy and Mam to get whipped because of me." A rush of tears blinded him and he let Old Juba turn him toward the door.

Quietly Old Juba said, "Sam came up to the house this evenin'."

Caesar's heart gave a jump. "Daddy did? To see me?"

"To get a look at you, if he could. He saw all the fuss goin' on in the kitchen, so he knew there'd be no chance you and he could talk."

"But he came to see me," Caesar said. "He wanted to see me as much as I wanted to see him."

"Think how lucky you are to be on the same plantation," Old Juba told him. "And remember, you both'll always be together in spirit."

"In spirit? What good does that do?"

"You'll find out as you grow older. Spirit's the best thing a slave can have. It's the one thing that no one can capture. Spirit's yours to help you through the bad times, the part of you that's free and that will always be free." He stepped close to Caesar and said, "Hold out your hands."

As Caesar obeyed, Old Juba handed him a jug filled with water. "If someone inside the house stops you, you've got a reason for goin' outside so late. Master Nathaniel's water jug's gettin' low, you tell 'em, and you want to be sure he won't get thirsty."

Still rebellious and wondering if he'd made a mistake and should have bolted down to the quarter, Caesar shut the door behind him and crossed the passage. Just for a few minutes he would have seen Daddy. He would have felt Daddy's arms around him. He would have snuggled into Mam's hug. He wouldn't have been gone long. No one would have missed him. Why hadn't he—?

The inside door from the passage suddenly opened, and candlelight shone in his eyes. "There you are!" Nat cried. "I didn't sleep well. When I woke and called for you, you weren't there! You disobeyed me. You were going to run—"

Nat stopped as he saw the jug in Caesar's hands. He stared, his mouth still open.

"Your water jug was almost empty, Master Nathaniel," Caesar said. "I'd forgotten to fill it."

"Oh," Nat said. He looked embarrassed. "Oh. Well, come back upstairs, then." The corners of his lips turned down, and he looked at Caesar as though Caesar had accused him of wrongdoing. " 'Tisn't easy being a master," Nat angrily complained. "My uncle reminds me I must be firm, I must learn to fulfill my duties. In less than twelve years this entire plantation will be mine, and I'll be obliged to manage it and every single slave on it."

Caesar looked down. "Yes, Master Nathaniel," he said.

Nat turned and walked slowly toward the stairway. His voice was low, as if he were talking to himself. "I know you wanted to see your father, but slaves are not like us. Uncle William has assured me, slaves don't have the same feelings we do. Their duty is to serve."

There was nothing Caesar could answer that would change Nat's mind. "Don't say all you see, and don't tell all you know," the old skeleton head in the forest had said. Caesar remembered and didn't speak.

"I—I'm sorry, Caesar," Nat said. Quickly he ran up the stairs. Caesar walked respectfully behind.

Caesar was glad Nat couldn't see his knees shaking. It had been close—*very* close. Because of what he had wanted to do, he would have been caught, and Mam and Daddy might have been whipped.

When they entered the room, Nat, who apparently still had a few doubts about Caesar's actions, walked directly to the stand at the side of the bed, held his candle high, and peered at it.

Caesar sucked in his breath. Nat would see that the water jug was there, filled with water. Caesar always kept it filled.

"From now on you will fill the water jug before I retire," Nat said. Without another word, he marched off to bed.

Caesar stepped closer to the stand. Amazed, he saw that there was no jug there. Someone must have taken—

He smiled. Old Juba had made certain Caesar wouldn't get into trouble. He'd removed the jug, then sat and waited in the dark for Caesar—maybe for hours. "Thank you," Caesar whispered, wishing Old Juba could hear him.

Chapter Eight

Caesar's favorite time of the day was early morning, when Mr. John Singer, one of the scholars from the College of William and Mary, came to Carter's Grove to tutor Nat before breakfast. Mr. Singer would perch on a chair next to the desk in the back parlor and teach Nat mathematics and history. Mr. Singer would also supervise Nat's progress in reading, writing, and penmanship. Although Caesar stood humbly and silently at one side, he listened intently to every word Mr. Singer said.

Caesar didn't try to understand all of the things Mr. Singer spoke about, but he was very much interested in the history lessons—especially when the topic of the wars of ancient Greece and Rome led to discussions of the war that was being fought with the French in the American colonies. Some of the battles taking place were not too far away, and Mr. Singer sometimes mentioned a man from Virginia, a Colonel George Washington. Colonel Washington had fought on the frontier. Now he was a burgess—a member of the legislature—and Mr. Singer considered him a man of great promise.

Caesar paid close attention to both Nat's and Mr. Singer's manner of speech. When he was alone he practiced speaking the way they did. And he read whatever and wherever he could. At night, while Nat was sleeping, Caesar read Nat's copybooks and practiced writing his letters and sums on Nat's slate.

Someday, Caesar promised himself, he'd speak like a gentleman and be able to read and cipher as well as any gentleman could. Then, if the time came for him to be free, he would be ready to live as a gentleman should.

One day, Nat seemed restless and distracted during his lessons. After Mr. Singer had left, Nat impatiently threw his copybook on the floor. "I'm weary of lessons," he complained. "It's a beautiful day. I'd rather be outside, riding."

"You will be riding. After breakfast you'll ride with

Mr. Nelson to inspect the tobacco crops," Caesar reminded him.

"I'd rather ride now," Nat answered. "Through the woods or down along the riverbank—not to inspect crops."

A summer breeze that drifted through the open windows ruffled the pages of the copybook on the floor. Caesar hurried to pick it up. He opened the book to the last page. On it Mr. Singer had written a list of questions that reviewed the lesson he had just given. He had instructed Nat to prepare the answers for the next day's recitation.

As Caesar handed the book to Nat he said, "Why don't I ask you the questions, Master Nathaniel? You can tell me the answers. That will help you when you recite your lesson tomorrow."

Nat thought a moment. "How long will it take?"

Eyes downcast, Caesar permitted himself a slight smile. "There aren't many questions. You'd be through before breakfast."

Nat still seemed dubious. "Are you certain you can read well enough to ask the questions?" he asked.

"Yes, sir," Caesar answered. Frantically he tried to think of an explanation. He couldn't tell Nat about the hours he spent reading after dark. He grasped at the first answer that came to him. "You helped me with reading when we were little children. Remember?"

"Proceed, then," Nat said. He handed the copybook to Caesar, then leaned back in the upholstered chair, stretching out his legs. "Ask the first question."

Caesar studied the words carefully, then read aloud, " 'Discuss the 1752 Treaty of Logstown.' "

Nat scowled. "Logstown? Logstown?"

Remembering Mr. Singer's earlier explanation, Caesar said, "It had to do with getting land."

Nat sat up. "Land south of the Ohio River. Am I correct?"

"You're correct, Master Nathaniel," Caesar said with enthusiasm. "But who was the land for? What company?"

"That's easy. . . . It was purchased for the Ohio Company."

Caesar nodded. "You're right again. Now, who signed this treaty?"

"The Colony of Virginia, of course," Nat said. He scowled and rubbed one thumb up and down his chin. "With Massachusetts?"

Quietly Caesar said, "I'm sorry, sir. I wasn't listening. I let my mind wander. You said, 'Delaware and the Iroquois Indians,' didn't you?"

"Umm, yes. At least, that's what I meant to say,"

Nat answered. He grinned, looking pleased with himself. "Continue, Caesar. What is the next question?"

Caesar read, " 'What was the first permanent British settlement in North America, and when was it established?' "

"Jamestown, in Virginia," Nat said. "Everybody knows that." He stopped and frowned again. "Why does Mr. Singer expect me to remember dates? How will that aid my education? Or help me someday to manage my plantation?"

"I'm certain you are right, Master Nathaniel," Caesar said, "which is why Mr. Singer won't expect you to know the date. But you'll fool him by shoutin' out, 'Sixteen-ought-seven!' and he'll be unable to complain to your uncle that you haven't studied."

Nat bent over, laughing. "A fine surprise for Mr. Singer, to be sure. Sixteen-ought-seven. I'll do it."

For a moment his eyes darkened, and his voice dropped. "I wish my father were still here."

Caesar nodded. "I'm sorry about your loss, Master Nathaniel."

Nat shook his head. "You mistook my meaning. Oh, I miss my father, to be sure. If it weren't for his portrait that hangs in the parlor, I think I might have completely forgotten what he looked like. Sometimes in the night I try to remember, and . . ."

Nat cleared his throat and continued. "What I meant was that I wish my father were here to govern Carter's Grove—not Uncle William and my other uncles, who all have their own opinions about what I am supposed to do." His words grew bitter. " 'You must learn to keep the accounts, Nathaniel.' 'You must take responsibility, Nathaniel.' 'When you have reached your majority this plantation will be yours, Nathaniel.' 'There is much you have to learn, Nathaniel.' I do not wish to be like my uncle William. I wish to govern as my father did."

Nat sighed. "Sometimes I would like nothing more than to run and play in the woods. Or to lie on the grass in the shade from the summer sun and watch the ships on the James River. Or to sit with my head against my mother's knee while she reads to me. But Uncle William has no patience with thoughts like these. He only becomes cross and reminds me that I have important duties to my family, those we employ, our slaves, and myself."

Caesar didn't know what to answer. He, too, longed for the life he had known as a small child. He hadn't found a way to regain those happy moments, so how could he help Nat to find a way? In the silence of the room an idea began to grow in his mind.

"Perhaps you could slip away—just for a few hours, until they missed you. We could go down to the fishing cove—just you and me. Trout should be jumping. Maybe we'd even catch us some perch or spot. Do you want to try?"

Unthinkingly Caesar had dared to look directly into Nat's eyes, and what he saw there frightened him. The agony that twisted Nat's features was suddenly swept away by scowling, tooth-clenching anger.

"Don't you ever dare to speak to me like that again," Nat commanded. "I am the master, and I will someday manage this plantation. I must resist temptation and accept my responsibilities."

He jumped to his feet and strode to the fireplace and back, head down, hands clasped behind his back. Frightened, Caesar could only think how much Nat resembled his stern uncle William.

Finally Nat stopped his pacing and turned to Caesar, who quickly dropped his gaze. "I have reminded myself that you are only a slave, Caesar. You have not the power to reason that I have. I must keep in mind my responsibilities to you, as well as to myself. You must never again speak to me as an equal, or—as Uncle William has promised—there will be a severe punishment. Can you understand?"

"I understand, Master Nathaniel," Caesar whispered.

Nat sighed. "I do not wish to have you beaten, Caesar. But I will if you can't learn what is expected of you and if you try to tempt me from doing what is expected of me."

"I—I'll learn, M-Master Nathaniel." Caesar tried to keep his voice from trembling, but he didn't succeed. He was terrified of being beaten, of being tied to the post while the lash bit bloody stripes into his back, then being cut down to crawl away in pain. He had seen it happen when Mr. Burfoot had required the slaves to come and watch. He had shuddered with each crack of the lash, hurting inside as though he himself had been wounded.

Nat let out a deep breath. He seated himself in his chair again and said, "Very well. We'll continue my studies. Ask me the next question, Caesar."

Slowly becoming able to control the shaking of his hands and voice, Caesar went through the list, asking about the current number of burgesses who had seats in the House of Burgesses—106—and the role of the present royal lieutenant governor of the Colony of Virginia.

"Francis Fauquier," Nat said promptly. "A good administrator, well liked, according to Uncle William. Lieutenant Governor Fauquier has visited Carter's Grove recently at the invitation of my uncle."

Caesar marveled that Nat could learn about a man in a lesson, then meet him in his own home. Nat didn't seem impressed. *Maybe that's another lesson I should learn,* Caesar thought. *Don't be impressed by people just because of who they are.*

Nat sat upright and held his left hand up, fingers spread. One by one he ticked off points on his fingers. "Francis Fauquier was appointed by the King to govern the Colony of Virginia. He doesn't have as much power as he would if he were governor instead of lieutenant governor. He has a council of advisors made up of twelve Virginians of the best families—including some of my own relatives—and one or two secretaries and clerks to assist him. But he has great influence."

Caesar put the copybook on the table. All the questions had been answered. "What does *influence* mean, Master Nathaniel? What is it?"

Nat smiled. "*Influence* is not a word you will have use for, but since you asked the meaning, I shall tell you. *Influence* means . . . um . . . well, that a man is thought of highly by others. His position and power

86

enable him to direct affairs of government. My father had influence. Someday I will have it."

Influence. That is a useful word I won't forget, Caesar thought. He cast his glance downward. "Thank you, Master Nathaniel," he said humbly.

Nat smiled, then jumped up and stretched. "It's near eight-thirty—time for breakfast," he said. He patted Caesar's shoulder, almost as a father would, as he added, "I will not tell Uncle William about your lapse this morning in learning the duties and behavior of a good personal servant. Yesterday he praised me for being a firm master and teaching you well."

As Nat paused, seeming to wait for an answer, Caesar said what he thought was expected. "I thank you, Master Nathaniel, for being a good teacher."

Whistling, Nat ran down the stairs to the dining room. Caesar walked more slowly to the kitchen, where he knew he would be given a wooden trencher filled with hominy—flavored with scraps of pork, if he was lucky. He smiled, knowing that since Patt, the cook, had taken a liking to him—saying he reminded her of her youngest son, who worked on the Foaces Plantation—he was even likely to find a dollop of molasses melting into the hot corn mixture.

His breakfast was just as he had expected, but he had to choke it down. He was still shaken by Nat's anger and his own mistaken lapse into the friendship they had once shared.

Caesar rinsed out his trencher and spoon and laid them on the table, where the dirty dishes would be stacked before washing. He walked to the woodpile and—careful of any shade-seeking spiders or snakes—picked out three cut logs to stack on the hearth in Nat's chamber.

Caesar began to walk toward the house, but Nat dashed around the corner, slowing to a dignified walk as he caught sight of Caesar.

"Hurry with the wood," Nat said. His eyes sparkled the way they once had when he knew a secret he was bursting to tell. "You must pack some of my clothes for a journey."

"A journey, Master Nathaniel?" Caesar almost dropped the logs. "Where are you going?"

"To Williamsburg with Uncle William. You're going, too, to care for my needs," Nat answered. His smile grew broader, and Caesar could see that there was more to the secret—a secret that it seemed Nat was going to keep.

Caesar stopped puzzling about Nat's secret as he realized that he was actually going to see the town of Williamsburg with its Courthouse and House of Burgesses and the Governor's Palace, where the lieutenant governor lived—all the places Mr. Singer had talked about. His heart gave an extra jump as he realized that he might even see his father—Daddy was working in Williamsburg! He didn't know where, but somehow . . . some way . . . he'd find him.

Chapter Nine

As Caesar carried Nat's portmanteau to the bottom of the back staircase, Old Juba pulled him aside. "You've never been to Williamsburg, child. There's somethin' I must tell you."

Caesar smiled at Old Juba. "Will you tell me where I can find my father? Is that it? Do you know?"

Old Juba slowly shook his head. "Don't be so impatient, child. They'll call for you soon, so listen to me. You may or may not be able to see your daddy. It don't matter. What matters is that you act good and proper."

Surprised, Caesar asked, "Don't I always? Well . . . almost always?"

"It's that 'almost' I'm thinkin' 'bout," Old Juba answered. "Things are done different in town. You tend to Master Nathaniel, and you remember to be respectful—not just to him, but to any white person you come across, no matter what."

Still puzzled, Caesar said, "I always am."

"Most town people aren't like the gentry who visit this house," Old Juba told him. "You'll find that—"

Cyrus, who drove the family's coach, stepped into the passage. Caesar had often seen Cyrus wearing his dark green livery of coat and matching breeches, but he thought again how fine Cyrus looked. "There you are," Cyrus said to Caesar. He grabbed the heavy portmanteau and easily swung it into his own large hand. "Hurry, boy. They're ready to leave."

Caesar, his small bundle tucked under an arm, trotted after Cyrus as with long steps he strode outside and around the house to the road, where the coach waited. Cyrus quickly fastened the baggage on the back of the coach.

As soon as Master Nathaniel and Mr. Nelson were handed up the steps and comfortably seated inside the coach, Cyrus closed the snug door. He and Richmond, the slave attending Mr. Nelson, quickly climbed onto the driver's outside seat.

Cyrus twisted to point at a place at the back of the

coach between the wheels. He said to Caesar, "Climb on there, boy, and hold tight. I try to keep the wheels out of the ruts and pits in the road, but if I hit one, I don't want you to fly off. I've enough to do managin' the horses without watchin' over you."

"I'll be careful," Caesar said. He gripped the metal handholds, prepared for the worst.

Cyrus was a good driver, Caesar decided, because he managed to miss the bumpiest spots in the dirt road. However, the place where Caesar stood on the coach was hard and narrow, the lumbering vehicle constantly jostled Caesar, and the trip took an hour. By the time they arrived at the outskirts of Williamsburg, Caesar was sore from head to foot.

As the coach rolled over the dirt streets, Caesar stared in amazement at the rows and rows of houses. Some, set close together, were small—as small as the house in which his family lived. And some were large—almost as large as the big house at Carter's Grove. There were gardens of vegetables, bright summer flowers, herbs, and blooming vines. Near some of the houses, trees created vast pools of shade with their widespread branches. Colorful painted signs hung outside some of the buildings, and Caesar tried to read and remember them all—even though he didn't know what some of the words meant. Milliner? Foundry? Apothecary?

What fascinated Caesar the most was all the people on the streets. Women with hats on their heads and baskets on their arms; men wearing fine waistcoats, breeches, and stiff black cocked hats; children of all ages; and slaves dressed much as he was dressed—all of them intent on where they were going or the persons to whom they were talking. Their voices blended into a murmur, buzzing around Caesar's ears like bees around a hive.

Caesar couldn't imagine living with so many people crowded together. How could they hear the music of the summer cicadas? The soft rustling of the breeze in the trees? The chatter of squirrels? Buzz, buzz, buzz . . . How could they shut out the noise so that they could think?

Two boys raced past, rolling their hoops and shouting, and two gentlemen stood under the sign of a tavern and loudly argued. Caesar was amazed at all he saw and heard.

From the way the morning sun hit his back, Caesar realized that they were traveling west. As the coach continued down the main street, Caesar saw that the buildings were spaced farther apart than those in the eastern part of the town.

They passed an open space with an eight-sided brick building surrounded by a brick fence on the left and another open area on the right. A few people were milling in both places. A white man and woman, dressed much like the slaves at the quarter, were packing vegetables in a cart. A boy and a man in similar clothing were leading a few sheep from the area, and a black woman was carrying away two baskets of squawking chickens. The grass looked muddy and trampled, the way the ground in the slave quarter and around the kitchen and laundry at Carter's Grove did.

As the coach turned right off the main street, Caesar looked approvingly at the wide strip of green lawn, dotted with trees, that divided the broad avenue they were now on. It wasn't at all like the view from Nat's window across the rolling hills to the James River, or the vista from the kitchen that overlooked the stretch of grass to the woods beyond. But the division on this street was equally handsome in its own way.

When the coach stopped in front of a large, impressive brick house, Caesar jumped from his place, quickly beat the dust from his clothing, and ran to open the coach door.

The wide front door of the house opened, and a

black man dressed much like the house slaves at Carter's Grove emerged. "Mr. and Mrs. Wythe invite you and Master Burwell to join them in the parlor, sir," he said to Mr. Nelson. "Please allow me to show you the way."

"Very well," Mr. Nelson replied. The man turned and led him and Nat up the stairs.

The door shut behind them.

"Get on," Cyrus instructed Caesar. Caesar hurried to his place on the back of the coach, and Cyrus urged the horses forward. They turned left and then left again, going through a gate that opened into the backyard of the house.

Richmond jumped down and began to unload the baggage. He handed Nat's portmanteau to Caesar, who gripped the heavy bag tightly. His own small bundle Caesar tucked under his other arm.

Anxious that he not make a mistake, Caesar whispered to Richmond, "Where do we go? What should we do?"

"You take Master Nathaniel's things to his room, and you do for him until he sends you to bed."

"Where do I sleep?"

"I'll sleep here in the back, in the laundry. You might, too. Or maybe Master Nathaniel will want you to sleep on the floor in his room. He'll tell you."

Caesar nodded. "I thank you."

Richmond grinned. "Don't look so frighted, child. Master Nathaniel's a good master. So is Master Nelson, compared to some masters I've seen. Come with me now."

Caesar struggled to catch up to Richmond, who strode toward the back door of the house.

"Richmond," a woman said as she stepped from a planting bed, one fist clutching sprays of herbs. "I'm mighty glad to see you here again."

Richmond grinned. "You look pretty as ever, Fanny."

As they chatted, Caesar studied the property with its large garden—larger than most he'd seen as the coach had rolled through Williamsburg. Scattered across the back of the property were a number of outbuildings. He wondered which one of them was the laundry, where Richmond and perhaps he would sleep.

Fanny led them down a path to the house and through the back door, into an elegant passage, and up the stairs.

"Your gentlemen will share this chamber," she told them. She stopped, hands on hips, and smiled at Caesar. "You're young to be a personal servant. They're trainin' you so early, you're bound to be a good one."

Caesar felt his face grow warm. Was Fanny teasing him? "There's much to learn," he said.

"Yes, there is," she answered. She turned to Richmond. "Too bad you wasn't here last Sunday evenin'," she told him. "We had a gatherin' down by the mill. Plenty of good music and dancin'. It's not very often we get time for ourselves."

"Come Christmas week the field hands will get their time for celebration," Richmond said. "The house servants will have some time, too. Maybe I'll come down to Williamsburg."

Fanny laughed. "Christmas seems a long time off. I'm not thinkin' that far ahead."

She tilted her head, listening. "Your gentlemen are on the way upstairs. You'll have plenty of work to ready them for dinner by three o'clock. Guests are comin'. We been cookin' for two days." Reaching for their personal bundles, Fanny said, "You'll be sleepin' in the laundry. I'll carry these out there for you."

No sooner had she left than Caesar could hear men's voices approaching. He looked to Richmond for guidance.

Richmond said softly, "Don't fear, child. You won't do anythin' wrong. Just do what you're told, that's all. Right now we'll unpack our masters' clothing."

A man dressed in fine clothes led the way into the

room. *This must be Mr. Wythe,* Caesar thought. He tried to shrink inside himself, becoming as small as possible as he laid out Nat's clothing on the bed, but it didn't matter. Mr. Wythe, Mr. Nelson, and Nat ignored Richmond and Caesar.

"Elizabeth has planned a fine dinner for us," Mr. Wythe said. "And there will be a few distinguished guests who are eager to meet you."

Mr. Nelson bent his head in a slight bow. "Our pleasure, sir," he said.

"One of them is Richard Taliaferro, Elizabeth's father and the talented builder of this house."

"We will be honored to meet him," Mr. Nelson said. "The design of your home interests me."

Mr. Wythe nodded. "Have you heard of Benjamin Powell, sir?"

"Indeed I have," Mr. Nelson answered.

"If you are interested in fine carpentry, then you might like to stop by the house he is building on York Street, just beyond Francis Street. Powell has formed a crew of the best carpenters he could hire—including some from outside Williamsburg—and the interior woodwork is much to be admired."

Caesar perked up, listening intently. The best carpenters? From outside Williamsburg? That description would have to include his father. Was that where

Daddy was working now? The house Mr. Powell was building on York Street?

Mr. Wythe continued. "In my opinion, the most distinguished feature of the interior is the pilastered archway in the stair passage."

Mr. Nelson cleared his throat. "I have much to learn about architecture, since it is not my main interest. I would rather hear more about your work with the law students at the College of William and Mary."

"The college. Ah, yes. Mr. John Blair, Jr., grand-nephew of the college's founder, will be with us, as will some of the instructors."

"Yes, I know Mr. Blair. I shall enjoy seeing him again," Mr. Nelson said.

Mr. Wythe pulled out his pocket watch, glanced at it, then stepped to the open doorway. "Will you and your nephew honor us with your presence down-stairs at three o'clock, sir?"

"It will be our pleasure, sir," Mr. Nelson answered.

Richmond closed the door softly, and he and Caesar helped Mr. Nelson and Nat wash and dress for dinner.

Caesar found the conversation during dinner so interesting he had to work hard to keep his attention on Nat's needs.

"The elections this summer have raised some questions among the students about voting regulations," one of the gentlemen said. "Some of them enjoy arguing a fine point."

Another gentleman put down his wineglass. "What are these questions?"

"They concern the criteria one must meet in order to vote," the first man answered. "The key qualification is the freehold—as we all know, a man who wishes to vote must own land, be leasing property for life, have a visible estate of fifty pounds, or be a freeman who was an apprentice in town for at least five years. We certainly do not want someone who does not have a stake in society to determine who will represent those of us who do.

"Second, we recognize that only men who are not dependent upon other persons can vote." One by one he ticked off on his fingers the items on his list. "This eliminates children, wives, servants, slaves, and Catholics, who we believe are dependent upon their church.

"Third, in order to be qualified to vote, people must have the capacity for self-control. This law makes sure that those who do not have the capacity—unmarried women, Indians, criminals, and the insane—are unable to vote."

"Your statement, sir, that some students question these regulations is very puzzling. What changes would they propose?" someone asked.

Mr. Wythe answered instead. With a chuckle he said, "No matter the rule or regulation, there are always a few young dissidents."

Mr. Nelson smiled. "Could it be that the dissidents fall into one of the categories of those not fit to vote?"

The men seated around the table burst into laughter.

Mrs. Wythe nodded graciously. "I will leave you to your port and pipes, gentlemen."

As she swept out of the room, the gentlemen stood courteously, then resumed their seats and began to talk about a few men with political ambitions who had money, but whom any true gentleman would consider nothing more than social upstarts.

Caesar, whose back was still sore from the bumpy coach ride, was thankful when Nat asked to be excused. Caesar followed Nat to the front of the house. Fanny, who had brought a bowl of strawberries to the parlor, quietly began to slip away, but Nat stopped her.

"Tell your mistress that I have gone for a walk," he said.

"Do you wish someone to go with you?" Fanny asked. "Someone who will know Williamsburg and help you find your way?"

Nat shook his head. "I can find my own way," he told her. "And I'll have Caesar with me."

"Yes, sir," Fanny answered, although her expression showed that she was concerned.

"We won't lose our way," Nat insisted. "My uncle will be busy for the next hour or so. We'll return by then."

Fanny curtseyed and left the room.

"Hurry, Caesar," Nat said. "Let's leave before she runs to get Mrs. Wythe to stop us."

It took only seconds for Nat and Caesar to bolt from the house. At the corner, next to a large brick church, Nat ran across the main street, dodging carriages and carts, and turned to the left. Soon they were so far away from the Wythes' house that no one would have been able to see in which direction they had gone.

The streets seemed busier in the late afternoon than they had earlier in the day. Twice Caesar was bumped by a laden basket. He walked cautiously, wondering how to avoid any further difficulties. There were too many people in Williamsburg, he decided.

Nat suddenly stopped in front of a building with the sign Wetherburn's Tavern. "There's a small shop across the street," he said. "Wait here for me, Caesar, while I'm inside the shop. I wish to find a gift for my mother."

"Yes, Master Nathaniel," Caesar said. He stepped into a spot near a pair of steps leading to the tavern's open doors, careful to stay out of the way of the patrons.

As he waited for Nat, Caesar thought about Williamsburg and how glad he'd be to go back to the quiet of the plantation. Personal slaves didn't have days off, as the field hands did, but sooner or later Nat might let him pay a visit to his mother. He could help her with her garden, maybe catch a mess of croaker, or an opossum, or . . .

Suddenly Caesar heard running footsteps, shouts, and laughter. He stepped out of his sheltered spot to see what was causing the commotion.

A large group of older boys—laughing and shouting—raced down the path toward Caesar. He tried to jump out of their way, but there was nowhere to go. He found himself swept up like a leaf caught in a whirl of dust and carried along until he tripped and fell to the ground.

Heedless, the boys ran on.

But the shouting became louder and deeper.

"There he is! That boy! Hold him!" a man yelled.

Caesar sat up and turned to see a portly, red-faced gentleman panting and struggling to pull himself up from the bottom tavern step.

As he got to his feet, the man furiously pointed at Caesar. "There's one of those ill-mannered ruffians!" he shouted. "He's the boy who stole my pocketbook!"

Chapter Ten

Hands gripped Caesar's shoulders, jerking him almost off the ground. "No, sir, I didn't!" Caesar cried as he tried to regain his footing.

Giving Caesar a shake, the man who held him growled, "Silence, boy!"

"Return my pocketbook!" the portly man shouted at Caesar.

"If you'll only listen for a moment, Mr. Moore, you'll find *I* am attempting to do exactly that," a woman called loudly.

Caesar looked up to see a plump, middle-aged woman standing on the top step, her hands on her hips. She glared at the portly man.

"Mr. Moore," she said, "that boy had nothing to do with the others who raced past here. I saw what happened. The boys ran into him and knocked him down, just as they did to you."

"But my pocketbook, Mrs. Wetherburn. It's been taken," Mr. Moore whined.

Mrs. Wetherburn raised one arm, letting the pocketbook dangle from her fingertips. "No one took it, sir. You dropped it inside, it was quickly found, and now I am returning it to you."

The fingers that had dug into Caesar's shoulders suddenly released him. Caesar didn't dare turn to see who had held him. He didn't even dare thank Mrs. Wetherburn. He stepped back into the sheltered corner between the steps and the brick wall, brushed the dirt off his knees and hands, and tried to make himself invisible. He had been badly frightened, and he was still shaking when Nat returned, a small package in one hand.

Nat held up the package. "A bottle of scent for my mother," he said. "She and my sisters like that kind of thing."

When Caesar didn't respond, Nat asked, "What was that shouting about? We could hear it inside the shop."

"Some boys ran by," Caesar said. He tried hard to keep his voice from trembling. "A man thought they'd stolen his pocketbook, but they hadn't. He'd dropped it in the tavern. The woman who owns the tavern brought it to him."

Nat studied Caesar. "Why are you so frightened?" he asked.

Caesar wanted to blurt out to Nat that the man had accused *him* of stealing his purse, but he could picture Old Juba's serious face and hear again the words Daddy had once said to him: "Don't say all you see, and don't tell all you know." Instead, he said, "There are too many people in Williamsburg, Master Nathaniel. I'll be glad when we're back at Carter's Grove."

The strange, mysterious twinkle returned to Nat's eyes, and his mouth twitched as he tried not to smile. "You may change your mind," he said.

Caesar took a deep breath. He had guessed that Nat was keeping a secret. Now he was sure of it. "Is there something you wish to tell me, Master Nathaniel?"

"Yes, there is," Nat said. "But not yet. Not until I'm sure of it myself."

Caesar knew it was not his place to ask. Though he

was curious about Nat's secret and concerned that he might be affected by it, he knew he would have to be patient.

Cautiously he followed Nat on his stroll through Williamsburg's streets. Nat pointed out a large brick building at the end of the main street. "Uncle William says that's the Capitol. That's where the House of Burgesses and the Council meet and the high courts are held. And the street we're on is called Duke of Gloucester Street."

Each street in Williamsburg had a name. One of the streets was named York. Mr. Wythe had talked about the house Mr. Powell was building on York Street. If they could walk along York Street, Caesar might learn whether his father was helping to build that house.

"Master Nathaniel," Caesar said, "do you know where York Street is?"

Nat stopped and tilted his head as he studied Caesar. "Why do you ask about York Street?"

Caesar took a deep breath and spoke quickly. "Because, sir, that's where the house is being built that Master Wythe spoke about. Your uncle said he didn't know much about architecture, but you're like your father, Master Nathaniel. I heard that Master Carter Burwell designed the house you live in, and he would have been interested in the house Mr. Powell is building . . . just like you would be."

"You're right. I'm more like my father than like my uncle," Nat said smugly.

"Master Wythe said that York Street was just beyond Francis Street."

"That's Francis Street just ahead of us," Nat said. He took a couple of steps in that direction, then abruptly stopped. "Look how long the shadows have grown. It will be dark soon. We've walked a long way, and Uncle will be angry if I don't return before dark."

Caesar kept himself from crying out in anguish. If he had guessed right, his father might be close by. If Daddy was there, and he could see him, maybe even speak to him, that was all he'd need to make him happy. They couldn't turn back now. "But the house—" he began.

"The house isn't that important," Nat said. He turned and began to walk briskly. "Come quickly, Caesar. Look—up there ahead, a merchant is already closing the shutters on his shop."

With a last look at Francis Street, Caesar silently followed Nat back to the Wythes' house.

"The Wythes live on Palace Street," Nat informed him importantly, "and the church on the corner is called Bruton Parish."

Caesar nodded politely, but he wasn't interested.

Once inside, Caesar helped Nat to wash. He brushed Nat's clothing and buffed his shoes. As Nat went downstairs to join the Wythes and Mr. Nelson, Caesar tidied his own clothing. Then he hurried out to the kitchen, where he was given a pewter spoon and a bowl filled with hominy.

Caesar gulped it hungrily, then returned to the house so that he would be ready when Nat called him.

At eight o'clock the Wythes served a light supper, which consisted of sliced meats, bread and butter, and sliced peaches. Caesar and Richmond stood quietly in the passage off the dining room, listening intently to the conversation.

Mr. Nelson seemed to be in a very fine mood. After a blessing was said over the food, he beamed at Nat. "You will be pleased to learn that you have been accepted at the college's grammar school. You will start classes there at the beginning of the next term and board at the college."

Caesar started in surprise. So this was Nat's secret. If Nat was to study at the College of William and Mary's grammar school, he would no longer be tutored at home. He would no longer live at home.

As he glanced cautiously through the doorway,

Caesar saw Nat give a bounce in his chair. "Did you see where I will live, Uncle?"

"Yes. The accommodations are on the upper floor of the college. They are plain but comfortable, and you will be under the watchful eye of a master and an usher. I am perfectly well satisfied, and I'm sure you will be, too."

Nat dropped his fork onto his plate. Caesar could see that he was too excited to eat.

"There are Indians at the college, Uncle!" Nat said. "Did you know that?"

Mr. Nelson nodded, and Mr. Wythe said, "Yes, but they are schooled in a different building and have their own curriculum, Nathaniel. They are being taught to live and behave like proper British gentlemen. It is our hope that when they finish their education and return to their tribes, they will take with them our manners and dress."

"A noble goal, sir," Mr. Nelson said.

He went on to instruct Nat in the subjects he would be studying, but Caesar stopped listening. *What will happen to me?* he wondered.

Chapter Eleven

After supper, Caesar helped Nat prepare for bed.

Grinning, Nat pulled off his breeches and tossed them to Caesar. "Well?" he asked. "What do you think of my news, Caesar? You haven't said a word about my coming here to Williamsburg to study."

"It makes you happy, Master Nathaniel," Caesar said, "so it must be fine." He gave a final brush to Nat's breeches, folded them, and laid them on a chair.

"Indeed, it does make me happy. I'm weary of tutors and living in a houseful of sisters. Of course, living at the college won't be as comfortable as my room at home. Also, I would have preferred to have you sleep on the floor in my room, but Uncle informed me that's not allowed because of lack of space. There is a room set aside for personal servants in the basement."

Caesar's mouth opened in astonishment. He dropped the shoe he was beginning to buff. "In the basement? Here in Williamsburg? Oh, no, Master Nathaniel! That can't be!"

Nat plopped onto the edge of the bed. His look of surprise quickly changed to one of annoyance. "What do you mean by saying no when I tell you what you will do?"

Caesar gulped down the fear that rose in his throat. Why was it so hard to remember not to speak out, not to blurt out his thoughts and feelings?

"I was just caught by surprise, Master Nathaniel," he said. He tried to compose himself. "I just meant to say I don't think you'd want me or need me here."

"*You* don't think? You have no right to think," Nat snapped. "I've told you before what Uncle William has taught me. I have the duty to think *for* you." His lower lip curled out in a pout. "You should be happy to come with me. As my personal slave, you should be grateful for everything I do for you."

Caesar stared down at the ground. He fought back tears, wishing he could rub his burning eyes. "I *am* grateful, Master Nathaniel," he said humbly.

"Then stop looking so miserable. Show how happy you are." Nat sighed. "You make it so hard for me to behave the way a master should."

"Yes, sir," Caesar said. He tried to smile, but a tear trickled down his cheek. Another one followed.

Nat frowned. "Now what's the matter with you?"

Caesar couldn't help it. He blurted out, "I don't want to live in Williamsburg, away from my family. I want to be with them at Carter's Grove."

"You'd go back to being a field hand, instead of caring for my needs?"

"Yes, sir."

Nat jumped off the bed, landing with a thump. He paced across the room and back while Caesar silently waited.

Finally Nat stopped. "You have a great deal to learn, Caesar, but I have, too. I must be patient. I must keep in mind the lessons Uncle William has taught me. Someday I'll be responsible not only for you, but for every one of the slaves at Carter's Grove. I am the one who will be obliged to decide what is best for them and make decisions . . . just as I must do now for you."

"Please let me go back," Caesar whispered.

"Let you go back to what? To being a small boy again? That's what you really want, isn't it—not the hard work in the fields? You'd like to run free each day with nothing to think about but filling your stomach when you're hungry."

"No! I—"

"Playing out in the fields and woods, fishing in the cove at the river. That's what you really want to go back to, but you can't." Nat's voice broke as he added, "And neither can I."

Caesar stifled a groan as memories of all that he had loved as a little boy painfully poured down on him. Under their weight it was hard to breathe, and his heart ached.

"I don't wish to hear another word about this matter," Nat said. "You have done well as my personal servant, and Uncle William has praised me for the way I have patiently trained you. I do not wish to look like a failure in his eyes, or to have to train someone to take your place, for which you may be thankful."

Caesar tensed at the anger in Nat's voice as he added, "Otherwise, I would persuade Uncle William to send you off to work as a field hand on one of the family quarters in Prince William County. There you would be so far from your family, you'd never see them again."

Nat, who had been his childhood friend, would do

this to him? Caesar shuddered as though a heavy stick had thwacked his shoulders. He trembled with anger. *I'll run away,* he thought. *I won't drown crossing the rivers, because I can swim. Maybe I'll hide on one of the ships that comes up the James River. They won't find me until we're well out to sea. I'll travel to other countries. I'll . . .* A sob suddenly tore at Caesar's throat. *I need my father,* he thought. *I'm going to find him.*

Numbly, his fingers feeling like blocks of wood, Caesar finished buffing Nat's shoes. He fluffed up Nat's pillows and turned down the counterpane on the bed. As always, he took care of Nat's bedtime ritual exactly the way Nat liked and expected, but his heart thumped and his head felt light and strange.

I'll run away, Caesar told himself.

Finally Nat climbed into bed. "Uncle will be here soon," he said. "You may be excused to go to sleep."

"Thank you, Master Nathaniel," Caesar said. He quietly made his way downstairs and out the back door.

Once outside, Caesar didn't go to the laundry. Instead, he silently hurried around to the front of the house, afraid to breathe in case someone might be there to hear him. When he reached Palace Street, he broke into a run. Retracing his steps in the full moonlight, he avoided the few people who were still out on the streets. Most of them were near the taverns, and Caesar—still shaken by what had happened with the tavern patron that afternoon—kept as far away from the doorways as he could get.

Finally he reached Francis Street. He continued east toward what he hoped was York Street.

Caesar stopped to get his bearings. He leaned against a tree, breathing heavily, and wondered where he could find his father.

Down the road, past a small house and a wide field, he saw a house under construction. A small pile of boards lay neatly stacked next to the house, and the yard needed planting. This must be the house Mr. Powell was building. Would Daddy sleep on the land? Or was there someplace nearby for the workmen to stay?

As Caesar came closer to the house, he caught the flicker of flames from a low bonfire in the field behind it. His heart pounding hard in excitement, he ran toward it. "Daddy?" he called.

His voice seemed so loud in the silence that Caesar took a step back, startled. But a figure rose in the darkness near the fire.

"Caesar? Is that you?"

"Daddy!" Caesar cried, and rushed into his father's arms.

For a few moments Sam held Caesar tightly. Then he stepped back, peering into Caesar's face. "What you doin' here?" he asked.

"I came to Williamsburg with Master Nathaniel and his uncle," Caesar said.

"And they let you come to see me? That was mighty kind of them."

"No, Daddy," Caesar answered. His voice shook as the words rushed out. "They don't know I came to see you. But I heard you were working on York Street so I hoped to find you. I have to tell you—"

"Later," Sam said. His voice was quiet but firm, and Caesar stopped talking.

"This is my son, Caesar," Sam said. Some of the shadows near the fire moved, and Caesar heard murmurs of greeting. He should have known that his father wouldn't be here alone.

"Let's walk," Sam said.

With only the moonlight to light the way, Caesar followed his father into the open field behind the street.

Finally Sam stopped and faced Caesar, placing his

hands on his shoulders. "Don't scold me for coming, Daddy," Caesar said. "I must talk to you."

Sam nodded. "Tell me what's troublin' you, son," he said.

Caesar began slowly and deliberately to tell everything that had happened and all that had been said, but as he talked about Nat's decisions for him, he grew more and more angry. "I don't want to live in Williamsburg, where I'll never see you or Mam or my sisters!" Caesar cried.

"You may not like what your master's got in mind for you, but you can't choose what you do," Sam said.

Angrily Caesar complained, "Nat doesn't understand that I want to be with my family. He said I was trying to get back to my childhood, and I couldn't." Caesar shivered. "Nat said I'd have to do what he said or he'd . . . he'd send me far away."

Sam put an arm around Caesar's shoulders and held him tightly. Caesar could feel the strong beating of his father's heart, and he clung to him. "Son, Master Nathaniel may be right," Sam said. "From what you tell me, you haven't started facin' what it's like to grow up."

Caesar looked up into his father's eyes. "Is growing up *giving* up?"

"Oh, no, son," Sam told him. "Growin' up means takin' stock of what you have and where you goin'. It means makin' plans to better your life and workin' to see those plans come to be. When I was a young man I knew I couldn't fight every white person in the colonies all by myself to get my freedom. And I knew I couldn't get enough other slaves to fight with me— not against men and horses and dogs and guns. But I decided if I couldn't be free, then I would at least make my life the best it could be. You know what I did."

"You learned how to become a very good carpenter," Caesar admitted. "But I—"

"But you what? Look at what you have, son. Look at where you are. Master Nathaniel is takin' you to a college, where people study and learn. You can pick up learnin' along with Master Nathaniel, as you've been doin'."

Still not convinced, Caesar murmured, "I could run away, Daddy."

"That'll bring you back to your family?"

"Well, no, but at least I'd be free."

"Free where? Not in any of the colonies. And if Indians catch you, you still not free. They either take you back to your master or make you their slave."

Caesar leaned against his father, exhausted. "There's no hope," he murmured.

Sam stroked the top of Caesar's head. "There's hope," he said. "Hope's in yourself. Learn to do somethin' so good that people will pay you to do it."

"Do what?" Caesar asked.

"That's for you to figure out. And you've plenty of time to do it. Right now you do what Master Nathaniel tells you, and figure out what you can learn at that college school."

Caesar sighed. "How can I learn? How can I even care about learning when there's nothing inside me but a big, black, empty hole?"

"It's not so empty in there. You got somethin' inside you that no one can take away," Sam told him. "Spirit. You got spirit."

Caesar frowned, remembering. "Old Juba told me once that I had spirit, and you and I would be together in spirit, but I don't understand what he meant. And I don't understand you, Daddy. What is spirit?"

There was silence as Sam thought a moment. Finally he answered, "Spirit is that light inside you that's always there. It burns as bright as you let it burn. It's yours and nobody else's, so if you hang on

121

to it, nobody can take it away from you, no matter what they say or what they do. Spirit will keep you strong, because that's the part of you that will always be free."

"Even if you can't do what you want to do?"

"Son, there ain't nobody—slave or free—can do everythin' he wants to do."

Caesar rested his head against his father's arm. "I promise you I won't run away, Daddy," he said, "but I wish . . . I wish . . ."

"You've no time for wishin'. You hurry back now to where you should be, before they start lookin' for you," Sam said. He gave Caesar a quick hug, then stood where he was, watching, as Caesar made his way across the field and back to York Street.

As he approached the Wythes' house, Caesar's mind was on his father and all that he had told him. His father was a good man, and he did his best for his family, taking on the responsibility of providing special things for them. Could he—Caesar—be that kind of man when he was grown?

As Caesar circled around to the back of the yard, behind the building where he would sleep, he heard voices. He turned the corner and saw Mr. Nelson, wearing a full-skirted banyan over his shirt. A sleeping cap perched on his head. Across from him, his gaze cast downward, stood Richmond.

"Where is that boy Caesar?" Mr. Nelson demanded. "If you've allowed him to run off, you'll be punished as severely as he!"

Caesar's voice was little more than a squeak as he stepped forward. "I haven't run off, sir," he said, his heart thumping. "Here I am."

Chapter Twelve

Mr. Nelson glared down at Caesar. "It's well for you that I needn't have gone looking for you. When your master calls you, you should be ready."

"Yes, sir," Caesar said. "What does Master Nathaniel want? I'll get it for him."

Mr. Nelson slapped a fist into the palm of his other hand. In the flickering lantern light he looked embarrassed. "He's had a bad dream," he mumbled. "Some childish thing. But he said he would sleep better if you were in his room."

"Yes, sir," Caesar said. "I'll go to him right away."

As he hurried into the house, following Mr. Nelson's long strides, Caesar was surprised to discover that his anger at Nat was completely gone. Instead he felt a strange kind of sorrow for his childhood friend, who woke so often with bad dreams no one could chase away. In many ways Nat—whose life was directed for him—was no more free than Caesar. What had Daddy said? There ain't nobody can do everythin' he wants to do.

Caesar made Nat comfortable, tucking the counterpane around him. Then he curled into a ball in a corner of the room, out of the way of Mr. Nelson, who grumbled and grunted as he climbed into his side of the bed.

Mr. Nelson soon began to snore, and Nat breathed in his sleep with a thin, whistling sound. Caesar was sure, with all that was on his mind, that he would not be able to rest. But the day had been exhausting, and in only a few minutes he fell into a deep sleep.

In the morning, after an early breakfast, Mr. Nelson and Nat climbed into the coach, ready for the ride back to Carter's Grove.

After they had been handed in and Richmond and Cyrus had climbed to the driver's seat, Richmond smiled at Caesar and held a hand down to him. "There's room up here with us," he said. "It's not so dusty, and you can get a good look at all the sights."

As the coach rumbled down Palace Street, Caesar

saw people heading south toward Duke of Gloucester Street. "Where are they going?" he asked Richmond.

Cyrus answered, "Market Square, to buy food at the market for the day's meals. We passed there yesterday."

Richmond squinted against the sun. "Somethin' else seems to be goin' on. Is there a fair today?"

"We're goin' that way so we'll find out," Cyrus said. He swung the horses left onto Duke of Gloucester Street.

Cyrus pointed to the eight-sided brick building Caesar had seen the day before. "That's the Magazine," he explained, "where the government keeps the colony's guns and gunpowder." He gestured toward the left. "Market Square is that open area in front of the Magazine and across the street from it."

As they approached Market Square, Caesar could see a group of people gathered around the steps of a tavern. On the broad top step stood three white men and several dark-skinned people.

Richmond muttered, "A slave auction. Let's get away from here."

But Mr. Nelson's voice called out from the open window below. "Stop here, Cyrus, where we can have a good view. There's a young, healthy-looking slave

126

ready to go on the block. I'd like to see how the bidding goes."

Cyrus pulled the horses to a stop so close to the steps that Caesar could see the terrible fear in the young man's eyes. What little clothing he wore was ragged and soiled, but he stood tall, shoulders back.

"That one's got spirit," Cyrus murmured to Richmond.

"Step up," the auctioneer commanded the slave. As he hesitated, the auctioneer motioned to a spot at the front of the steps.

The auctioneer jabbed the slave in the ribs, and he jumped forward. But he turned to look behind him, where an older woman stood with tears pouring from her eyes.

A cry escaped Caesar as he saw the woman's pain. "Is that his mother?" he whispered.

Richmond clamped a hand on Caesar's shoulder. "Don't say anythin'. Don't even let yourself think anythin'. There's nothin' you can do that won't get us all in trouble."

Wincing against the grip that dug into his shoulder, Caesar nodded, and the pressure from Richmond's fingers eased.

Half a dozen men, dressed in fine suits, wigs, and cocked hats, crowded close to the slave. One reached up to examine the young man's muscles. One asked the assistant to show the slave's teeth.

Caesar pressed his hands against his stomach, sick and terrified at what he was seeing. He couldn't stop looking at the people huddled together on the step. Most of them were adults, but there were a few children. One was a girl who was probably Caesar's age. She stood close by a boy, half her size, her arm around him, and the fear on her face tore at Caesar's heart.

The girl made him think of his mother. The vision of his mother being sold at a slave auction was so real it was unbearable. Was this the way it had happened to Mam? A horrible thought struck Caesar. Maybe these children had already been taken from their parents, brought to a new and strange land without a mother or father to love and care for them, the way it had happened to Mam so long ago. Silent tears ran down Caesar's cheeks. He didn't try to rub them away.

At last the auctioneer called for bids, and the sale began.

The bidding quickly rose to an amount Caesar marveled at. Was that what a strong young male slave was worth?

Caesar heard Mr. Nelson complain to Nat, "Too

high. The bidding is much too high. We have no more time to waste here."

As Cyrus slapped the reins, urging on the horses, Richmond whispered to Caesar, "Did you see the hard faces on some of those buyers?"

Caesar shivered and nodded. He was so shaken by what had happened that he couldn't speak.

"Master Nathaniel is a good master," Richmond said. "He'll never be as cruel as those men could be. Be grateful for what you have."

The horses, at Cyrus's direction, picked up speed, and the coach was soon headed toward Carter's Grove and home.

Home for only a little while longer, Caesar thought sadly. Soon he'd be living in Williamsburg.

He wiped his sleeve across his eyes and twisted in his seat, looking back at the tidy houses and gardens on the outskirts of Williamsburg.

I'll be careful. I'll do my job well. And I'll remember what I've learned. That old skeleton head won't get me.

Richmond glanced down at Caesar and asked, "Are you all right now?"

"Yes, I am," Caesar answered. He realized that his voice sounded stronger, perhaps even a little deeper. "I've made some plans for my future."

Richmond grinned and tried to wink over Caesar's

head at Cyrus. "Think about all those dark-skinned people you saw on the streets in Williamsburg," he said. "Every one of 'em was busy goin' and comin' just because somebody ordered 'em where and how to go and come. Slaves don't make plans. They don't determine their own futures."

"That's not what my father told me," Caesar answered. "He made plans for his future, and I will, too. As soon as I'm old enough, I'll learn a skill. Maybe I'll work at Carter's Grove. Or maybe Williamsburg, with all its jobs and people, will be the place where I'll find what I'm best fitted for. I'll be so skilled at what I do that I'll be hired out, and I'll make good use of every bit of the wages Master Nathaniel lets me keep—like my father does."

Caesar felt a surge of strength that warmed his chest. He sat up straighter and held his shoulders back. He would stop clinging to childhood and grow up, as he should. And he'd make a good life for himself and for the people he loved. He knew. . . . He could feel it—that light they called spirit. He had it.

Epilogue

When Molly Otts had finished her story, her listeners were silent.

Finally Lori spoke up. "I don't understand how people could convince themselves that slavery was right," she said. "It was cruel. It was unfair. It was a terrible way to treat other human beings."

"Slavery took away people's dignity," Keisha said. "Imagine how awful it would be to be put on an auction block and examined as if you were a horse."

Halim slowly shook his head. "I always knew that slavery was a bad thing, but I never tried to think how my great-great-great-grandfather must have felt, being a slave. I wonder if he ever wanted to run away. I wonder if he ever felt like giving up."

Keisha put a hand on Halim's arm. "You're here because he made a life for himself," she said. "I think your great-great-great-grandfather must have been like Caesar. I think he had spirit, too."

"Did Caesar really live at Carter's Grove?" Stewart asked.

"Oh my yes," Mrs. Otts answered. "His birth and baptism were recorded, and the Colonial Williamsburg Foundation still has copies of the old records."

Chip said, "In your story you told us that Caesar saw words that were new to him on some of the signs in Williamsburg. Like *apothecary* and *foundry*. In the last story Ann McKenzie's father had an apothecary. Was that the same one Caesar saw? And remember— Ann's friend, John Geddy, was part of the family that owned the foundry. Was that the same foundry, or was it a different one?"

"The apothecary was not the same. Dr. Kenneth McKenzie died in 1755," Mrs. Otts answered. "But the foundry was the same Geddy Foundry.

"As a matter of fact, if you're here tomorrow morning, I'll tell you about Nancy Geddy, who was twelve years old in the year 1765. Nancy's father, James Geddy, was brother to the John Geddy I told you about. James learned silversmithing from Samuel Galt, a Scottish immigrant who rented property from James's mother.

"But 'tis Nancy Geddy I want to tell you about. A fine young girl, with talents to spare, but she and her stepmother didn't always see eye to eye. Her closest friend was her grandmother, Anne, and together they . . ."

Molly Otts stopped speaking, and Lori asked, "Together they what? What did they do?"

Mrs. Otts smiled, and her eyes twinkled. "That would be telling too much," she said. "Come back early tomorrow, and I promise you'll hear Nancy's story."

Author's Note

We know very little about the lives of individual slaves in Colonial Williamsburg. There are only a few exceptions.

We know that Caesar was born in the spring of 1750, and that he lived and worked at Carter's Grove plantation. We also know that later Nathaniel Burwell listed an adult slave named Caesar, a barber who lived at Carter's Grove, and we believe the two Caesars may have been the same person. We know nothing about Caesar's childhood and growing-up years. We can only imagine what he might have done and might have dreamed.

It is possible that Caesar could read. Carter

Burwell may have believed that all his slaves should be baptized in the Anglican Church. Some may have learned how to read well enough to learn the church's catechism. Although later, in the 1800s, it was illegal to teach slaves to read in Virginia, in the 1700s Virginia law did not prohibit slaves from reading.

In 1760, the Bray School, sponsored by an English organization dedicated to improving conditions within the institution of slavery (but not ending it), was opened in Williamsburg for the purpose of teaching young slaves, both boys and girls between three and ten years of age, to read the Bible, to write, and to learn the *Church Catechism*. Girls learned to knit, and everyone was taught how to act during church services. Mrs. Anne Wager served for fourteen years as the Bray School mistress, and Robert Carter Nicholas oversaw the operations of the school.

We don't know what kind of relationship Caesar and Nat had. We do know that after they grew up, Nat sometimes loaned a slave named Caesar small amounts of money. Nat also borrowed coins, which were scarce, from some of his other slaves. We also know that as late as 1806, the barber named Caesar was living at Carter's Grove.

Sam was a carpenter at Carter's Grove who

belonged to Nathaniel's father and then to Nathaniel. There are records that show Sam was hired out. Belinda, Milly, Sukey, and Nell were also slaves from Carter Burwell's estate who lived at Carter's Grove around the middle of the 1700s. They may or may not have been related to Caesar, but we have borrowed their names to give to Caesar's family.

The other Carter's Grove slaves in the story all lived at the plantation around the mid-eighteenth century. A slave named Fanny was living and working in George Wythe's household in 1759.

Historians must look at many kinds of records to learn about the lives of slaves in colonial Virginia. As mentioned earlier, births, baptisms, and purchases of slaves were frequently recorded. Sometimes when slave owners bought or sold a slave, they wrote in their account books—books that show how much they earned and spent—how old the slave was and what job he or she did. Some owners noted how much it cost to feed and clothe their slaves.

A few account books tell how much money an owner received for hiring out a slave and how much of that money—if any—the owner let the slave keep, while others tell who hired slaves and what jobs they had them do. Some also show that Williamsburg housewives bought vegetables, eggs, chickens, baskets, and other items from slaves. Store accounts reveal what slaves bought with the money they earned.

The names of slaves who were tried for crimes, and their punishments if they were convicted, can be found in court records. A handful of cases tell us about owners who harmed their slaves. Runaway slave advertisements in colonial newspapers often mention how old a slave was, what kind of work the runaway did, the clothing he or she wore, and, sometimes, where the slave's family lived or where the runaway came from originally.

Slave owners and their families sometimes mentioned slaves in their diaries and letters. A few freed slaves wrote autobiographies. Archaeologists have excavated items slaves owned and bones that tell us what kind of fish and animals the slaves ate. And some rare items that slaves made have survived for more than two hundred years to become valuable collectors' items.

When we combine the information we have learned from these many sources, we get an idea of what life was like for slaves in Virginia in the 1700s.

There is more information available about Nathaniel Burwell. Nathaniel was born on Easter Sunday, April 15, 1750, close to the time when Caesar was born.

Nat's father, Carter Burwell, and his mother, Lucy Grymes Burwell, had nine children. Nat was seventh in line, the first boy to be born to Carter and Lucy. Imagine having *six* older sisters!

When Carter Burwell died, Nat was only six years old, but his father had left Carter's Grove plantation and many acres of land elsewhere in Virginia to him. Nat was destined to take complete control of the plantation when he became twenty-one in 1771.

Robert Carter Nicholas, half brother of Carter Burwell, was named guardian of all Carter Burwell's children, but records show that William Nelson, who had married Carter Burwell's sister Elizabeth, took over the position of guardian and acted as executor of Carter Burwell's estate. We do not know whether the Burwells were living at Carter's Grove in 1759. There is evidence that Mrs. Burwell moved the family away from the plantation sometime after her husband died, but there is no way to find out exactly when.

Nat studied at the College of William and Mary from 1759 until 1772 and was considered a good student. He received the degree of Bachelor of Arts, and at the graduation ceremony both he and James Madison, a fellow student who later became the bishop of Virginia and president of the College of William and Mary, were awarded gold medals.

After Nat's graduation, his uncle William turned over to him the duties of administering Carter's Grove and the other lands Nat had inherited. Nat married Suzanna Grimes and raised a family of six children at Carter's Grove.

Benjamin Powell lived in the house he built on York Street until around 1763, when he bought another house near the Capitol. The second house is called the Benjamin Powell House today and is sometimes open to visitors to Colonial Williamsburg.

About
Williamsburg

The story of Williamsburg, the capital of eighteenth-century Virginia, began more than seventy-five years before the thirteen original colonies became the United States in 1776.

Williamsburg was the colony's second capital. Jamestown, the first permanent English settlement in North America, was the first. Jamestown stood on a swampy peninsula in the James River, and over the years, people found it an unhealthy place to live. They also feared that ships sailing up the river could attack the town.

In 1699, a year after the Statehouse at Jamestown burned down for the fourth time, Virginians decided to move the capital a few miles away, to a place

The Capitol at Williamsburg

known as Middle Plantation. On high ground between two rivers, Middle Plantation was a healthier and safer location that was already home to several of Virginia's leading citizens.

Middle Plantation was also the home of the College of William and Mary, today one of Virginia's most revered institutions. The college received its charter from King William III and Queen Mary II of England in 1693. Its graduates include two of our nation's first presidents: Thomas Jefferson and James Monroe.

The new capital's name was changed to Williamsburg in honor of King William. Like the Colony of Virginia, Williamsburg grew during the eighteenth century. Government officials and their families arrived. Taverns opened for business, and merchants and artisans settled in. Much of the heavy labor and domestic work was performed by African Americans, most of them slaves, although a few were free. By the eve of the American Revolution, nearly two thousand people—roughly half of them white and half of them black—lived in Williamsburg.

The Revolutionary War and Its Leaders

The formal dates of the American Revolution are 1775 to 1783, but the problems between the thirteen original colonies and Great Britain, their mother country, began in 1765, when Parliament enacted the Stamp Act.

England was in debt from fighting the Seven Years War (called the French and Indian War in the colonies) and believed that the colonists should help pay the debt. The colonists were stunned. They considered themselves English and believed they had the same political rights as people living in England. These rights included being taxed *only* by an elected body, such as each colony's legislature. Now a body in which they were not represented, Parliament, was taxing them.

A reenactment of Virginia legislators debating the Stamp Act

All thirteen colonies protested, and the Stamp Act was repealed in 1766. Over the next eleven years, however, Great Britain imposed other taxes and enacted other laws that the colonists believed infringed on their rights. Finally, in 1775, the second Continental Congress, made up of representatives from twelve of the colonies, established an army. The following year, the Congress (now with

143

representatives from all thirteen colonies) declared independence from Great Britain.

The Revolutionary War was the historical event that ensured Williamsburg's place in American history. Events that happened there and the people who participated in them helped form the values on which the United States was founded. Virginians meeting in Williamsburg helped lead the thirteen colonies to independence.

In fact, Americans first declared independence in the Capitol building in Williamsburg. There, on May 15, 1776, the colony's leaders declared Virginia's full freedom from England. In a unanimous vote, they also instructed the colony's representatives to the Continental Congress to propose that the Congress "declare the United Colonies free and independent states absolved from all allegiances to or dependence upon the crown or parliament of Great Britain."

Three weeks later, Richard Henry Lee, one of Virginia's delegates, stood before the Congress and proposed independence. His action led directly to the writing of the Declaration of Independence. The Congress adopted the Declaration on July 2 and signed it two days later. The United States of America was born.

Williamsburg served as a training ground for three noteworthy patriots: George Washington, Thomas Jefferson, and Patrick Henry. Each arrived in Williamsburg as a young man, and there each matured into a statesman.

In 1752, George Washington, who later led the American forces to victory over the British in the Revolutionary War and became our nation's first president, came to Williamsburg at the age of nineteen. He soon began a career in the military, which led to a seat in Virginia's legislature, the House of Burgesses. He served as a burgess for sixteen years—negotiating legislation, engaging in political discussions, and building social and political relationships. These experiences helped mold him into one of America's finest political leaders.

Patrick Henry, who would go on to become the first governor of the Commonwealth of Virginia as well as a powerful advocate for the Bill of Rights, first traveled to Williamsburg in 1760 to obtain a law license. Only twenty-three years old, he barely squeaked through the exam. Five years later, as a first-time burgess, he led Virginia's opposition to the Stamp Act. For the next eleven years, Henry's talent as a speaker—including his now famous Caesar-Brutus speech and the immortal cry, "Give me liberty or give me death!"—rallied Virginians to the patriots' cause.

Thomas Jefferson, who later wrote the Declaration of Independence, succeeded Patrick Henry as the governor of Virginia, and became the third president of the United States, arrived in Williamsburg in 1760 at the age of seventeen to attend the College of William and Mary. As the cousin of Peyton Randolph, the respected Speaker of the House of Burgesses, Jefferson was immediately welcomed by Williamsburg society. He became a lawyer and was elected a burgess in 1769. In his very first session, the royal governor closed the legislature because it had protested the Townshend Acts. The burgesses moved the meeting to the Raleigh Tavern, where they drew up an agreement to boycott British goods.

Jefferson, Henry, and Washington each signed the agreement. In the years that followed, all three men supported the patriots' cause and the nation that grew out of it.

Williamsburg Then and Now

Williamsburg in the eighteenth century was a vibrant American town. Thanks largely to the vision of the

Reverend Dr. W.A.R. Goodwin, rector of Bruton Parish Church at the opening of the twentieth century, its vitality can still be experienced today. The

The Reverend Dr. W.A.R. Goodwin with John D. Rockefeller, Jr.

generosity of philanthropist John D. Rockefeller, Jr., made it possible to restore Williamsburg to its eighteenth-century glory. Original colonial buildings were acquired and carefully returned to their eighteenth-century appearance. Later houses and buildings were torn down and replaced by carefully researched reconstructions, most built on original eighteenth-century foundations. Rockefeller gave the project both money and enthusiastic support for more than thirty years.

Today, the Historic Area of Williamsburg is both a museum and a living city. The restored buildings, antique furnishings, and costumed interpreters can help you create a picture of the past in your mind's eye. The Historic Area is operated by the Colonial Williamsburg Foundation, a nonprofit educational organization staffed by historians, interpreters, actors, administrators, numerous people behind the scenes, and many volunteers.

Williamsburg is a living reminder of our country's past and a guide to its future; it shows us where we have been and can give us clues about where we may be going. Though the stories of the people who lived in the eighteenth-century Williamsburg may seem very different from our lives in the twenty-first century, the heart of the stories remains the same. We created a nation based on new ideas about liberty, independence, and democracy. The Colonial Williamsburg: Young Americans books are about individuals who may not have experienced these principles in their own lives, but whose lives foreshadowed changes for the generations that followed. People like the smart and capable Ann McKenzie in

Ann's Story: 1747, who struggled to reconcile her interest in medicine with society's expectations for an eighteenth-century woman. People like the brave

A scene from Colonial Williamsburg today

Caesar in *Caesar's Story: 1759,* who struggled in silence against the institution of slavery that gripped his people, his family, and himself. While some of these lives evoke painful memories of our country's history, they are a part of that history nonetheless and cannot be forgotten. These stories form the foundation of our country. The people in them are the unspoken heroes of our time.

Childhood in Eighteenth-Century Virginia

If you traveled back in time to Virginia in the 1700s, some things would probably seem familiar to you. Colonial children played some of the same games that children play today: blindman's buff, hopscotch, leapfrog, and hide-and-seek. Girls had dolls, boys flew kites, and both boys and girls might play with puzzles and read.

You might be surprised, however, at how few toys even well-to-do children owned. Adults and children in the 1700s owned far fewer things than we do today, not only fewer toys but also less furniture and clothing. And the books children read were either educational or taught them how to behave properly, such as *Aesop's Fables* and the *School of Manners.*

Small children dressed almost alike back then. Boys

and girls in prosperous families wore gowns (dresses) similar to the ones older girls and women wore. Less well-to-do white children and enslaved children wore shifts, which were much like our nightgowns. Both black and white boys began wearing pants when they were between five and seven years old. Boys and girls in colonial Virginia began doing chores when they were six or seven, probably the same age at which *you* started doing chores around the house. But their chores included tasks such as toting kindling, grinding corn with a mortar and pestle, and turning a spit so that meat would roast evenly over the fire.

These chores were done by both black and white children. Many enslaved children also began working in the fields at this age. They might pick worms off tobacco, carry water to older workers, hoe, or pull weeds. However, they usually were not expected to do as much work as the adults.

As black and white children grew older, they were assigned more and sometimes harder chores. Few children of either race went to school. Those who did usually came from prosperous white families, although there were some charity schools. Some middling (middle-class) and gentry (upper-class) children studied at home with tutors. Other white children learned from their mothers and fathers to read, write, and do simple arithmetic. But not all white children were taught these skills, and very few enslaved children learned them.

When they were ten, eleven, or twelve years

old, children began preparing in earnest for adult-hood.

Boys from well-to-do families got a university education at the College of William and Mary in Williamsburg or at a university in England. Their advanced studies prepared them to manage the

plantations they inherited or to become lawyers and important government officials. Many did all three things.

Many middle-class boys and some poorer ones became apprentices. An apprentice agreed to work

An apprentice with the master cabinetmaker

for a master for several years, usually until the apprentice turned twenty-one. The master agreed to teach the apprentice his trade or profession, to ensure that he learned to read and write, and, usually, to feed, clothe, and house him. Apprentices became apothecaries (druggist-doctors), blacksmiths, carpenters, coopers (barrel makers), founders (men who cast metals in a foundry), merchants, printers, shoemakers, silversmiths, store clerks, and wig makers. Some girls, usually orphans with no families, also became apprentices. A girl apprentice usually lived with a family and worked as a domestic servant.

Most white girls, however, learned at home. Their mothers or other female relatives taught them the skills they would need to manage their households after they married—such as cooking, sewing, knitting, cleaning, doing the laundry, managing domestic slaves, and caring for ailing family members. Some middle-class and most gentry girls also learned music, dance, embroidery, and sometimes French. Formal education for girls of all classes, however, was usually limited to reading, writing, and arithmetic.

Enslaved children also began training for adulthood when they were ten to twelve years old. Some boys and girls worked in the house and learned to be domestic slaves. Others worked in the fields. Some boys learned a trade.

Because masters had to pay taxes on slaves who were sixteen years old or older, slaves were expected to do a full day's work when they turned sixteen, if not sooner. White boys, however, usually were not considered adults until they reached the age of twenty-one. White girls were considered to be adults when they turned twenty-one or married, whichever came first.

Enslaved or free black boys watching tradesmen saw wood

When we look back, we see many elements of colonial childhood that are familiar to us—the love of toys and games, the need to help the family around the house, and the task of preparing for adulthood. However, it is interesting to compare the days of a colonial child to the days of a child today and to see all the ways in which life has changed for children over the years.

Slavery in Colonial Virginia

In 1619, a Dutch ship brought a small group of Africans to Jamestown, Virginia. Historians at Colonial Williamsburg believe that these men and women, the first black people known to have been in the colony, were enslaved.

Most laborers in Virginia in 1619 were indentured servants. An indentured servant worked for a master in exchange for passage to the New World. After several years, the servant received his or her freedom.

Because a slave system had not yet developed in Virginia, some settlers treated the early Africans as indentured servants. Black indentured servants, like white ones, eventually received their freedom.

The settlers needed labor, so more Africans were brought to Virginia. Slave traders, both African and European, kidnapped men, women, and children

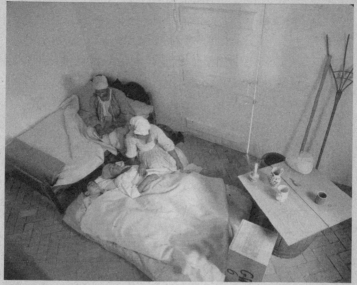

Domestic slaves in the outbuilding where they live

from their tribes. They transported them like livestock in the holds of ships. Many slaves died during the journey. White settlers bought those who arrived in Virginia.

Over time, the way white Virginians treated Africans and their offspring changed. The legislature began to pass laws that restricted the rights of black people. By the last quarter of the seventeenth century, most black Virginians were enslaved. The majority were agricultural workers. The rest worked as domestic slaves or tradespeople.

Many Virginian households did not own slaves. Those that did usually had only one or two. Most slaves, like most whites, lived on farms. Slaves often lived in the same houses as their owners, but they were not considered equal to the members of the owner's family.

A few wealthy Virginians owned many slaves. Domestic servants lived in the owners' houses or nearby outbuildings. Farm workers usually lived away from the main house in an area called a quarter.

As Molly Otts explains at the beginning of Caesar's story, most whites and blacks in colonial Virginia lived under the same kinds of conditions. Many white people did the same kinds of work as black people did. But slaves were not free.

A slave's owner decided where a slave would live. The owner determined what kind of work a slave would do. The owner could beat a slave or subject him or her to other punishments on a whim. The owner decided whether a slave's family stayed together or was separated.

A slave could be sent to work for someone else, the

way Caesar's father was. A slave might have to work on a distant farm, as Nat threatened to make Caesar do. Slaves could be given as gifts, as Milly was afraid she would be given to Nat's sister.

Domestic slaves cleaning at the Raleigh Tavern as the tavern keeper supervises

Against the background of this inequality, slaves developed a rich culture that helped them cope with and resist slavery. Religion, music, and dance eased the burdens of hard labor and separation from loved ones. Storytelling taught black children about their heritage and showed them how to interact with white

An enslaved boy learning to make baskets

people. Old Juba reminds Caesar of the moral of one story: "Don't say all you see, and don't tell all you know."

Some slaves protested poor treatment through their actions. They might work more slowly than usual or claim to be sick.

Some slaves tried to escape. Many, however, chose not to run away. Slavery was legal in all thirteen colonies, so there was no safe place to go. Being caught was always a danger. For many slaves, leaving family and friends was too high a price to pay for freedom.

The slaves played vital roles in colonial Virginia. By the time of the Revolution, blacks made up more than forty percent of Virginia's population. More than half of the people in Williamsburg were black. Historians continue to learn how slaves affected the colony's economy, social structure, and culture. Caesar's story brings to life what researchers have discovered so far.

Colonial Williamsburg Staff

Recipe for Bean Hominy

Corn was a staple in the diet of most colonial Virginians. Besides eating fresh corn in the summer, the colonists used ground corn year-round to make a number of dishes. Many ate hominy, a boiled cereal made from coarsely ground cornmeal, for both breakfast and dinner (the main meal of the day, served about two in the afternoon).

The colonists called hominy with beans in it bean hominy and hominy with fish or meat in it great hominy. They might also add fresh or dried vegetables to it.

164

1½ cups coarsely ground cornmeal
1 can kidney beans (about 15 ounces), drained
1 quart water

Combine the ingredients in a saucepan and bring to a boil. Lower the heat and simmer (so that bubbles come gently to the surface), stirring frequently. Cook about 30 minutes, or until the mixture has thickened to the consistency of oatmeal or cream of wheat. If your cornmeal is very coarse, you may have to cook the hominy longer.

You can also combine the ingredients in a slow cooker and cook the mixture for 6 to 8 hours. Serves 6.

Recipe developed by Colonial Williamsburg Staff